I screamed and screamed and screamed.

I heard my own cries, heard the animal terror of my friends, their jibbering, babbling cries of horror.

Was I on my knees? *Stand up. Run! Run, Jalil.*

But I could not stop screaming. A sound came from me that I could not make. Couldn't. Could I? That hideous, nightmare howl? Was that from me? . . .

She was dead. She was death itself.

Her flesh was the color of raw concrete. Gray. Ash. But with spots of color like bruises: yellow and green and purple.

Her eye was an empty socket, dark as the cave she'd come from. The left side of her nose was eaten away, gnawed down to the cartilage. There was a rip in her cheek, revealing the rotting, gumless teeth in her mouth. Her tongue writhed with worms that lived within dead flesh itself. . . .

"Her face," I said in a shaken whisper to the others. "Look away from her face. . . ."

Look for other EVERWORLD titles

by K.A. Applegate:

#1 Search for Senna
#2 Land of Loss
#3 Enter the Enchanted

EVER WORLD

REALM OF THE REAPER

K. A. APPLEGATE

SCHOLASTIC INC.
New York Toronto London Auckland Sydney
Mexico City New Delhi Hong Kong

ISBN 0-590-87760-7

Copyright © 1999 by Katherine Applegate.
All rights reserved. Published by Scholastic Inc.
SCHOLASTIC and associated logos are trademarks and/or registered trademarks of Scholastic Inc.
EVERWORLD and associated logos are trademarks and/or registered trademarks of Katherine Applegate.

12 11 10 9 8 7 6 5 4 3 2 1   9/9 0 1 2 3 4/0

Printed in the U.S.A.

First Scholastic printing, November 1999

For Michael
and Jake

REALM OF THE REAPER

CHAPTER
I

I washed my hands.

Stood at my sink in the bathroom I use, the one down the hall, upstairs, my bathroom, my sink, and washed my hands.

Over there, in Everworld, I was asleep. Over there I had just fallen to the ground out in the open, the soggy fire barely warming the parts of me that were closest to it, not touching the far side of me. Over there I had glanced at David — he had first watch, he always had first watch — then laid down on damp ground, on what few twigs and grasses I could assemble into a laughable bed, and then fallen asleep.

Over there, over in Everworld, I was filthy. Over there my body crawled with the fleas, lice, and ticks I'd picked up during our last indoor night's sleep.

Here in the real world I finished washing my hands. Turned off the faucet. Put down the soap. Tried to walk away. Told myself I could walk away. Of course I could walk away.

I began washing my hands again.

I was there. I was here. I was him, I was me, I was we, a plural, living two lives, two wildly different existences, all with the identical brain, the identical body, me, always me, and yet . . .

I turned off the faucet. I put away the soap. I tried to walk away. I had washed my hands five times. Five. Five was four too many. I knew that. I wasn't insane, I knew I had washed my hands five times, knew it was unnecessary, knew it was absurd, ridiculous, worst of all, irrational.

But seven was the number. Seven. Not five. Seven was safe. Had to be seven. No reason. Why even ask? There could not possibly be a reason. People washed their hands once. In an entire day, maybe twice, three times. They had lives, normal lives, they didn't die, they weren't eaten alive by bacteria.

But there was no point resisting. I'd already gone to five. Two more and I would be free, for a while. Seven. That was the number.

I lived here. I lived there. But only here did the dark, ritual impulses rule me. Only here. Why? This was the world of reason. This was the world where cause and effect were always cause and effect; they did not reverse order.

This was the world that could be added and subtracted, divided and multiplied, where circles were functions of pi, where all objects fell at the same constant rate of acceleration, where laws of physics were laws, not suggestions.

This was my world. The world of two plus two equals four every time. No wizards, no witches, no dragons, no trolls, no gods and goddesses. My world, understandable, decipherable, logical.

But it was here, here in this world that I stood helpless at my sink, and washed my hands again because the number, you see, is seven.

Over there, in Everworld, in that mad place, that lunatic asylum, that universe where gods feed on human hearts, where wolves could grow to the size of city buses, that universe of dragons where Senna Wales had drawn me, over there I could lie asleep, aware of the itching of fleas, aware of the dirt under my fingernails, aware of the filth all around me, and still sleep.

Over there, in the place where nothing made sense, seven was not the number. There was no number. Obsessive-Compulsive Disorder. That's what it's called. OCD. Or just OC. A brain wired to learn learns some things too well. A brain wired to eliminate threats becomes fixated, staring endlessly at a threat that is no real threat at all. I knew what it was called. I'd read all about it. Knew the illness, knew the enemy. But I did not know how to make it stop.

Only once had I felt peace here in the real world. Only once had the compulsion disappeared. Once, and only for a moment, I had regained control only to discover that I had lost it after all.

Once. Because of Senna Wales.

I washed my hands a seventh time. I would be free, for a while.

And over there, another me, but still me, would eventually wake up wearing filthy clothing and not wash at all, but eat a crust of black peasant bread with dirty fingers.

CHAPTER
II

"Is that a pig?"

"Yeah. I think so."

"It has tusks or something."

"Yeah? Well, we have swords. And we're hungry."

Two weeks in the forest. Two weeks of walking along trails that came and went, appeared and disappeared, and never seemed to lead anywhere.

Two weeks of water slurped up from fast-rushing streams. Two weeks of eating whatever we could find: berries, wild onions, squirrels, acorns. Two weeks of unwashed clothing and unchanged socks and underwear that cried out for a can of lighter fluid and a match.

We were dirty. We smelled. We were four nasty teenagers in lousy moods.

For the last three days we'd lived on the black

peasant bread and wormy, shriveled apples that had been our last paycheck. Back at a little village of about forty men, women, and children with roughly seven teeth between them. Stunted, gnarled, scabby, scruffy examples of what happens when chromosomes go sour.

But they liked our little minstrel show. They liked April's singing, they liked Christopher's jokes — didn't laugh at them, but liked them. They tolerated our dance number. They listened with rapt attention as I told them stories. Fairy tales, pretty much: Snow White. Hansel and Gretel. Br'er Rabbit. President Clinton and Monica Lewinsky.

It was all new to them. No Uncle Remus, no Aesop, no Mother Goose, no MSNBC.

They gave us a roof over our heads for two nights, right in the home of one of the village's more prosperous citizens, a man with one large bed on the floor. A bed shared by him, his wife, his three sons, his two daughters, his three pigs, his goat, his cow and her calf, and however many chickens cared to climb in.

And the four of us. One of the daughters flirted with David, Christopher, and me, each in turn, though not necessarily in that order. Some instinct, some evolutionary imperative to please, please locate some new DNA. She was turned down three times.

The next day they left us with some loaves of bread, the apples, each about the size of a Ping-Pong ball, a sort of wad of rancid cheese, and all the fleas, ticks, lice, and bedbugs we could carry. Everyone had already seen our act twice. And if we weren't going to contribute anything more personal, well, they didn't have a long-term need for minstrels.

"I hope you know I am not cooking that pig. I am not going to cut the guts out of some wild pig," April protested a little shrilly. "Bad enough I have to eat meat here, I am not removing organs. I'm a vegetarian."

"Maybe we better take this in order," I suggested. "Kill first, then worry about the barbecue sauce."

"Shh. Don't scare him off," David warned.

"He's not scared," Christopher said.

"No. He's not, is he? Why isn't he scared?"

"Maybe he can't see us."

"Well, Jalil, he can sure as hell smell us."

"Here, piggy, piggy, Daddy wants some bacon," David said.

And then the pig was moving. Not running away. Rushing us. Fast.

David raised his sword to his shoulder, Sammy Sosa waiting for a fast one down the middle.

The pig ran. David swung. The pig hit him

hard. David spun and fell, clutching his leg and crying out in pain. I saw a splash of bright red.

Christopher yelled a curse and then the pig was on me. I stabbed downward at it, missed, stuck my sword point in the ground, no time to yank it back out, the pig knocked me down like a bowling ball hitting the last standing pin. I landed hard. The pig was on me. I shoved. Hands against muscle, not fat. Fingers pushing against sharp, prickly fur.

The tusks, the curved, nasty teeth, that snout, inches from my face. The pig was going to rip my face open. The pig was going to kill me.

Christopher swung his stick like a club. It slammed down on the pig's spine. The pig grunted. Shoved its face closer to mine. I cried out. No words, just a desperate, scared wailing sound.

Christopher stabbed at the pig. Nothing.

But then, quite calmly, the pig climbed down off me. It trotted about six steps, then paused, turned, and looked at us with amused contempt.

Then the pig said, "Give me your apples. Give me your apples or I'll gut you, one by one."

We gave him our apples.

Just another day in Everworld.

Chapter
III

Here is what I understand of Everworld. It doesn't amount to much, and I may be mistaken in many of the details.

Everworld is a universe. Small, perhaps, relative to our own. In Everworld we see the stars at night, the moon rises and sets, the sun seems to be the sun we all know, but I suspect that the sun and moon and stars are not real. Not as we know reality. I do not believe the stars, these stars, are huge suns, millions of light-years distant. I suspect they are an illusion.

What is real in Everworld is the land and water around us. How big it is, whether it is an actual, spherical planet in orbit around an actual sun, I don't know. It may not be round at all. It may be flat.

Thousands of miles across? Tens of miles? Millions of miles? We don't know.

How it came into existence? Well, the story is that the ancient gods of Earth, the myths, the Zeuses and Odins and Isises and Quetzalcoatls all got tired of life on good old planet Earth and decided to make themselves a new place. A new universe where they wrote all the rules.

How long ago? No one says. How did they go about the job of creating a universe? No one says.

What seems to be true, however, is that Everworld is an actual place. Of necessity a different universe because the immutable rules that exist in our own universe seem to be rather flexible here.

Things still fall downward. But maybe not at a fixed rate of acceleration.

There is still cause and effect, except that sometimes there is effect without any real cause. And it's only a matter of time before I see some cause without effect.

There is magic here. Not Siegfried and Roy. Real magic. I've seen an old man chant some words and cause cooked, half-eaten, definitely dead deer and pigs and quails and sheep to roll over off the dishes, jump up, and go on the attack.

I've seen it. It's real. It pains me to say that because I do know the difference between myth and reality, between mumbo-jumbo superstition and the truth that comes from experiments performed and recorded and then repeated.

An old man muttering a rhyme cannot cause a dead deer to move. Not in our universe. Not anywhere in our universe. Not a million light-years from Earth on some far-distant planet.

So Everworld is a different universe. Different rules. It runs on different software.

But that isn't the end of the Everworld story. They say that this cozy "gods and their subjects only" universe was invaded by the gods of other planets and peoples. Like someone guessing the right keyword to break into a private chat room.

Fine when it was the relatively harmless gods of the Coo-Hatch. Not so fine when it was Ka Anor, god of the Hetwan.

Ka Anor: the god eater.

Now Loki and others want out of Everworld fast, before Ka Anor gets hungry for them. Merlin wants to unite the gods to resist Ka Anor. And it all comes down to possession of Senna Wales, the gateway between universes.

We are four high school kids from a suburb north of Chicago. Not friends. Acquaintances, but with a connection. Drawn together one morning, down to the lake to see Senna, a girl we all knew. The four of us and Senna were dragged out of our universe into Everworld by a wolf the size of a three-car garage.

The Fenris wolf: Fenrir. Son of Loki, the Norse god of chaos and destruction.

We were carried along in her wake. We woke up to find Senna gone, and the four of us chained to the outer walls of Loki's castle.

Welcome to Everworld, Jalil Sherman.

Four of us: David Levin, a wannabe hero. And maybe a real hero, who knows? He stepped up when he had to. Maybe that's the definition of a hero. He's a dark-eyed, dark-haired white boy with a thing for Senna, some of which is natural attraction and some of which is Senna doing the things she can do to people.

Christopher Hitchcock, a big, dumb surfer dude, except he isn't really dumb. I haven't figured Christopher out yet. I'm good at ideas, good at abstractions, not so good at people. At times he was like my best friend. A second later he was this racist jerkwad. Brave, cowardly, stand-up, self-centered. One minute he'd take your hand, the next slap it away.

Like I said, I didn't get him.

April O'Brien is the only girl. Woman. Young woman. I understood her, well enough at least.

She's my opposite in lots of ways, in terms of ideas, anyway. She looks like someone's idea of a poster girl for Irish-American day: auburn hair, green eyes, a mocking smile that manages to be sexy and smart-aleck little sisterish all at once.

I was in a debate once with April, in a speech class almost a year ago. The topic was faith versus reason. I won the debate on points. She got the votes of every kid in the class except two.

And finally, there's me. Gangly, wiry, skinny, pick your adjective. I prefer lean myself. A black poindexter, most people think. Jalil, that's my name. People assume it's an African name. It's not. It's Hindi, and it means "godlike."

Sometimes irony takes a while to develop.

That's the four of us. Four lost, ignorant, scared kids trying to find Senna and get home, and stay alive, and maybe, somehow, change the fate that seemed to be aiming the two universes for a collision that would unleash all the horrors of Everworld upon a planet with more than enough horrors already.

Would Loki and his ilk have their powers in the real world? He seemed to think so. I didn't think he intended to move to Chicago and get a job at the nearest car wash.

So many questions. So many uncertainties. It

was a great big toy store of mysteries. And I would have enjoyed figuring it all out. On CD-ROM. In some game.

But the real Everworld was full of real death. From gods and wizards, dragons and trolls. And over it all loomed the still unseen, but ever-present threat of Ka Anor.

But, hey, in Everworld you could get killed by a talking pig.

Chapter
IV

The day after the pig.

Hungrier, dirtier, madder, more confused than
ever. Still clueless. And now the forest, which had
always been dark, was getting darker. The trees
taller. The canopy more impenetrable. Or maybe
the sun had just been turned off. Maybe that was
it, because the light that made it through the
trees down to us might as well have come from a
forty-watt bulb.

So dark. So quiet. So empty. The squirrels and
birds were gone. No one had seen a deer since the
day before.

Strangest of all, the path was improving. It was
clearer, easier to stay on. You could look ahead
and see it winding away like a Disney version of
a forest trail. Where the old trail would have me-
andered around large rocks, this path seemed to

have been cleared of them. There were small, split-log footbridges over the frequent, tiny streams. At least we had plenty to drink. And we kept our feet dry.

We came to a river. The path led to the left along the riverbank. Thirty yards along there was a shallow ford. The water simmered, white around rocks, chuckling and rippling over the riverbed, resting in pools before plunging on ahead.

There was a clear way across. A dozen large, flat rocks placed in such a way that any reasonably agile person could jump from one to the next. The rocks baked dry in the first sunlight we'd seen in a long time.

From where we crouched, in the shade of a low-hanging willow, peering through the vine-like branches, we could not see the far side of the ford. The trail of rocks cut around past an over-hanging tree before, presumably, reaching the far shore.

I blinked, stared, shaded my eyes with my hands. My eyes watered, no longer accustomed to adjusting to bright light.

"This feels bad," April said. "Gives me the willies."

"Yeah," David agreed. "I'm getting a bad read

off this. Have been for a while. Just a bad feeling.
Like someone watching us."

That annoyed me. "It's not a bad feeling.
You've just observed incongruities."

"Here it comes," Christopher muttered.

"We've been on a trail that was clearly made by
the passage of animals, later followed by men. It
seems to be made naturally. It comes and goes, it
weaves in and out. Then suddenly we find ourselves on a trail that is obviously deliberately
tended. Then this ford, which is not an accident.
Those rocks were placed here. That's why you feel
strange."

"Like I said, gives me the willies," April said
with a dazzling smile for me.

"This has 'trap' written all over it," David said.
He pointed across. "If I'm looking to snag some
travelers, I wait right over there, out of sight on
the far bank. We're forced into the open, highly
visible."

"That's right, G.I. Joe," Christopher agreed.
"You better go on ahead and do some recon. We'll
catch a snooze. Let us know if you get killed or
anything, okay? Hut! Hut! Move out, Marine!"

"We need to cross somewhere else," David insisted, ignoring the ridicule.

"Why do we need to cross at all?" Christopher

demanded in a loud, exasperated voice. "We're lost. I mean, are we following Senna at this point? I don't think so. Are we looking for Ka Anor to kick his big alien ass? I don't think so. We are wandering around lost in the forest, going nowhere, starving, scratching our flea-bit butts, dealing with talking pigs, and hoping Loki doesn't find us and feed us to his trolls."

"You want to go back?" David snapped. "Back the way we came?"

David takes it personally when anyone questions our actions. Like he's responsible. Even though major decisions involve all of us. It seems foolish to me. By taking offense he basically accepts responsibility.

Christopher was perfectly happy to let David bear the blame. "Yeah, I want to go back, find the talking pig, and convince him to come back to the real world with me. You have any idea how much money a talking pig would be worth?"

I couldn't let him get away with that one. "It may have escaped your notice, Christopher, but we can't get back to the real world, with or without a talking pig."

"So let's keep going forward," April said. She winked at David. "I feel great forces guiding my steps to find another crossing. I sense the cosmic rightness of this direction. I believe it may involve the attraction of a crystal, or possibly just fluctuations in my own magnetic fields."

I laughed. She was trying to provoke me, of course.

"If you're in touch with the Great Cosmic Fluctuating Crystal, see if you can get directions to a nice Hyatt Regency. I'd kill for a shower and fresh sheets."

"Kill who?" Christopher asked.

"Don't worry, Christopher, I wouldn't kill you for a shower. I'd kill you for a breath mint."

"Let's head upstream," David said. "If someone's watching this ford they could sweep downstream in canoes and catch us crossing."

"Canoes?" I echoed.

David shook his head helplessly. "I don't know, Jalil. I'm just trying to cover every angle, all right?"

"Canoes, hell, they could come after us with killer mermaids, or singing freaking sea serpents, or windsurfing leprechauns. W.T.E.," Christopher said.

W.T.E. Welcome To Everworld. It had become our all-purpose phrase.

The others had mostly given up trying to make sense of Everworld. April pretty much just accepted the notion of magic. But then again, she'd grown up in the church and shared a home with Senna.

Christopher wasn't interested in understanding; he just wanted a cold drink and a way home. And a talking pig, so he could sit in a lawn chair somewhere and sell tickets at five bucks a pop.

David might have cared, only I don't think he wanted to look too deeply at anything.

Me? I knew that there were rules underlying all we saw and experienced. Things make sense, once you know the rules. That was the human experience: that mysteries evaporate if you pay close enough attention.

You want control? Learn the software.

We trudged back into the forest and began pushing our way upstream. It was hard going with no trail at all. Our feet sank into sucking mud and we slapped ourselves raw trying to ward off a cloud of some tiny, black flying insects. An hour's hard march moved us no more than two hundred yards from the ford.

"It'll be getting dark in a couple hours," David said. "We should do this while there's light. I think we'll be hidden from their sight."

" 'Their,' " I muttered. "Like we know who 'they' are. Or if there even is a 'they.' "

We waded out into the water. The cold was

shocking but not unwelcome. It soothed the flea bites on my legs a little. Maybe it would even drown a few of the little monsters.

I walked out a few steps, then let myself sink under the surface. I scrubbed my head with my fingertips, scrubbed my face, then came back up.

Cold. Very cold. My ears hurt. My fingertips were getting numb. The force of the current tugged at my clothes. My sneakers crunched on rock and shifting gravel. The water was up to my chest, higher for April.

I pushed toward her. "Take my hand."

"Thanks."

We pushed forward together. I could feel her being floated up and away from the riverbed.

"Maybe we'd better swim for it," David called back. "Deeper than I thought."

He was already paddling, resisting the current, breaststroking parallel to the riverbank. I held on to April's hand and focused on not letting go.

Then, I stepped into nothing. My foot plunged down, my body after it. My cry was cut off as ice water filled my mouth.

I lost my footing entirely and was swept away, unable to swim effectively because April still clutched one hand. It seemed to take forever to surface. My lungs burned.

The weight of the sword on my hip was dragging me down. The weight of water filled my clothes, my shoes. I let go of April's hand, no choice.

I kicked hard and reached air, sucked it in, tried to look around, get my bearings, find April, but water was in my eyes and nose and mouth.

"April!"

I tried to fight the current, but no, that was wrong, what if April was floating downstream? I had let go of her. Should I follow her?

I kicked my sodden, lead-weight shoes and tried to gain altitude to see around me, see over the ripples and rolls of white water.

Then, I hit. A rock. In the lower back. It knocked the wind out of me. I choked, tried to breathe, sucked in water.

Fear. Now I was afraid. I fought the urge to breathe again, to suck more water into my lungs. I twisted, tried to come face-to-face with the rock, but then I was free, floating head forward like the tip of a spear that would be driven into the next rock.

Air! Forget everything else, get to the air. I swam, frantic, but now everything was twisted around. Which way was up?

Something grabbed me. I felt a kick in my shoulder. I twisted around. Whatever held me shifted grip. Air! I sucked in a breath.

April's hands kept their grip on my shirt. She drew me up toward her. Not strong enough to haul me clear of the water, but she kept my face up and my head away from the sharp edge of rock.

I twisted, slapped my palms down on the rock, did a push-up, and lifted my upper body onto the rock.

April squatted beside me. She pushed the wet hair out of her face. I drew myself up into a sitting position.

"Thanks."

"No problem, Jalil."

I looked for David and Christopher. They were sitting together, looking about as drowned as April and I. We were all back at the ford, about midstream.

"Hey, I have a suggestion," Christopher yelled to us. "Let's cross right here."

CHAPTER V

We saved our weapons. Saved our shoes and clothes.

We lost the last of our food.

We stuck to the path and were not ambushed. That fact made us feel a little foolish about nearly drowning ourselves.

We followed the path, which now was even wider and more unobstructed than before.

"It's clearing out up ahead there. I saw some actual sky," Christopher said.

"Yeah. Maybe this forest has an end."

We trudged on. "Definitely clearing. Maybe a meadow," I said.

The path turned a sharp left, dodging around a huge, gnarled live oak tree. I turned, looked down, looked up, and yelled, "Whoa!"

The trail ended very suddenly. Like we'd been walking across a sheet cake and someone had cut a slice. There was a sheer drop. A cliff, though not terribly high.

The ground below the cliff sloped down and away from us. A landscape of lichen-scabbed rocks and grass that was almost blue in color. The ground swept down and down to meet the river, which had curved back this direction. Or else was an entirely different river. Most likely a different river because the waters of this one were almost black. Loaded with silt, maybe. Like when you see flood runoff on TV.

On the far side of the river was a hill. It was almost perfectly triangular.

It didn't look right. Didn't look natural. More like some huge slag heap that had been partly overgrown with grass and twisted dwarf trees. The lower third of the hill's face was nothing but blasted rock. A gray-black scar on an unhealthy face.

Crowding behind and shouldered up beside it were more natural hills, still steep but natural, with scatterings of wildflowers and tumbled rock and the asymmetries that are part of any natural geography.

There was a look of poison about that first hill.

Maybe some subterranean spring of tainted water. Maybe some sort of Everworld toxic-waste
dump. Something.

At the base of the hill, on the near side of the
black river, was a town. Much bigger than the village we'd stayed in. This town had walls surrounding it pierced by only a single gate.

Five towers formed the walls into a rough,
elongated pentagon, though there were few really
straight lines. Far down the wall, to our left, a
monstrous pile of refuse and, quite likely, sewage
lay against the wall. A person could very nearly
climb that foul mess and make it over the wall.

Careless of the people within the walls.

A stumpy castle consisting of two square towers and a square keep dominated the center of the
town. I saw no soldiers on the battlements. No
flags flew from the keep.

My first impression was that the castle itself
was abandoned. Maybe, maybe not. But the town
was alive enough. I saw an ox-drawn cart and
driver. A scattering of people in the half-dozen
twisting, winding streets. No doubt there were
more; that was all I could see over the walls.

"That is not a Hyatt Regency," April said.

"Yeah, but see that, out beyond the walls? The
smoke? That outbuilding?" I said, pointing to a
whitewashed stone building that bulged out from

the wall, thankfully far from the refuse pile. "I believe that's a bakery."

"Why do you say that?" David asked.

"These people are still stuck in the Middle Ages. In those days they built communal ovens outside of the town. Different bakers would bring their bread loaves there to bake them."

Christopher shot me a look. "And you just pulled this interesting fact out of your butt, or what?"

"I spend some of my real-world time doing research," I said.

"You would."

"They put the bakery outside the town so the ovens won't be a fire threat. Fire's a big problem."

"Bakery, that means bread," David said. "We need food. But I get a bad feeling off this place."

"Like you did off the river?" I said skeptically. "These people are about a thousand years behind the twenty-first century. Everything they do is going to look grim to us."

I said this, made all the right noises, but inside me I felt what David felt. Dread.

David shrugged. "Doesn't matter much, anyway. We have no choice. We need food."

"Let's go check it out, then. What are we? Minstrels again?" Christopher asked.

"We could tell them we're selling magazine

subscriptions door to door," David said. "But I think the minstrel thing works for us."

We found stairs cut into the cliff face. Someone had made it awfully easy for us.

Once down the cliff we began crossing the open field, dodging the rocks, tripping over concealed holes and gullies overgrown with grass. For some reason the trail failed at this point. Maybe it wasn't deemed necessary.

Closer to the city we went. Closer to the competing smells of freshly baked bread and rotting garbage. Closer to the black river and the looming hill with its scar-tissue face.

Bread smells good when you're starving. Bread smells very good when you've handed over your last food to a murderous talking pig.

We approached the single gate. It was open. Maybe not unusual since it was broad daylight. But it was also unguarded. Definitely not usual. Not for the medieval mentality. Not usual for a city with a fortress at its core. A medieval city was a military as much as a civic entity.

Not that this was truly the Middle Ages. This was Everworld, I reminded myself. This was not medieval France or England or Italy.

Closer now I could see people moving near the bakery. Half a dozen, carrying wooden boards that might in turn be loaded with individual loaves. They were moving strangely. Carrying the heavy loads with one hand. Using the other hand to hold on to a rope line stretched between the various whitewashed buildings. What did it mean?

"Okay. What's the tune?" David asked.

I tore my gaze from the strange bakery workers. I gritted my teeth. "Man, I hate this. It's so embarrassing."

"This" was the minstrel walk.

"It's advertising," April said.

"Yeah. I know. And I have no problem with the concept of advertising. I just don't want to be in it. I'm not Ronald McDonald."

"Are you the Taco Bell Chihuahua? Because I love that dog, man," Christopher said. "Are you the Energizer Bunny?"

He was in a good mood now because I wasn't. Somehow Christopher and I had become polarized. Like opposite ends of a magnet. If I was positive, he was negative.

"Something peppy and upbeat," April said. "Something we all know this time, so you guys don't peter out on me after the first two lines."

"I know 'Happy Birthday,'" Christopher suggested.

"Yeah, that would be good," David said. "We're minstrels, not morons."

We were still walking, still nearing the gate. We'd be there in a few minutes. The dread was not lessening. We all felt it. Irrational, yes, but hard to ignore just the same.

"Here's a story, of a lovely lady, who was bringing up three very lovely girls . . ." April sang. "What? No Nick at Night fans here?"

"How about you, Jalil? Do you know any songs? Maybe something involving 'bustin' a cap on da ho'?"

Christopher, of course. I decided to let the barb sail by unnoticed. This time.

"I don't care much about music," I admitted as I scanned the gate ahead.

"You have a nice voice when you bother to sing and not just mouth the words," April said. "Come on. You must know something."

"There may be guards just inside the gate," David said, shading his eyes with his hand. "Can't be sure."

"Yeah. Thought I saw a flash of armor. My dad's the musical one," I said. "Used to be a musician in his wild days of youth. Played bass."

"I didn't know that," April said.

"Definite guard, inside right. But he's not paying attention to us."

"They're blind!" I blurted.

"Who? Who's blind?"

"The people back at the bakery. They're feeling their way around on a rope line."

David looked troubled. He strained to see the bakery, but we were in a dip of the land and in any case we were close enough now that the bulge of a tower half hid the bakery.

"Maybe that means they're civilized," April said. "You know, hiring the handicapped."

"No," I said.

"Hey, we need food. So let's go in singing and frolicking," Christopher said. "They won't mess with us if we sing and frolic."

I was poised between two worlds. Seeing the gate. Determined not to let a sense of foreboding affect me.

And at the same time remembering my dad, back when I was maybe five or six, having these old men over to the house to play. They'd be skinny, dried-up, worn-looking men. Men with tracks inside both elbows. Men with their nose eaten away by a lifetime of hard drinking. Men with watery eyes behind dark shades, and Salvation Army clothes.

Blues men.

Some were blind.

Blind bakery workers. Why? Because the blind are better bakers? No. Because they were outside the walls? And if so, what did that mean?

"What was that song?" April asked.

"What?"

"You were humming. Come on. We're almost there. We cannot enter the city singing 'Happy Birthday.'"

Closer. Closer. Chatting about music. David providing running commentary on the height of the walls, the position of the towers, the absence of guards.

We were no more than a city block away from the gate. It was three times the height of a man, maybe eight feet wide. Massive trapezoidal stones formed the arch. There was a drop-gate of pointed wood stakes. The gate was up and suspended.

And there were definitely two guards. Big men. One white guy with lots of long blond hair. One, a black man. Both wearing what might be Viking armor, though it was hard to tell. Real Vikings don't wear those Hagar-the-Horrible horns.

The guards were glancing over their shoulders at us. Surprised. Maybe even grimly amused. But each time they spared us only a glance before returning their gaze inward.

Something was wrong with that. Very wrong.

"They're keeping people in," I said.

CHAPTER
VI

"You're right," David said. "This is some kind of . . . prison or whatever."

"Let's turn around and sing and frolic our way the hell out of here," Christopher said.

He turned. So did I. And at the same moment we saw the column of men marching toward us, coming up from the south, but definitely heading for the gate.

Six men on horseback wearing black-and-silver armor, except for a bronze plate over their hearts.

"It's the Oakland Raiders," Christopher said.

The six horsemen were guarding twenty or so men, yoked neck to neck. Only on closer examination the "men" weren't all human. Some were very definitely not human.

David cursed. "Not that way."

The column was moving along at a good clip

now, hurrying to reach the city. At least the horsemen were in a hurry. I heard the crack of a whip.

"If we're going in, we want to walk in," April
said. "As minstrels. Not as whatever those guys
are."

"She's right," Christopher said. "But I vote we
don't go in at all. Those two guys at the gate,
man, they're laughing at us."

I shot a look up, past the relatively puny walls
and towers of the town. Up at the mountain. It
was impossible to shake the feeling that the
mountain itself was somehow watching me.

I shook off that thought and focused on the
problem at hand. "Simple: Those guards up there
know we shouldn't be walking into that town.
They know more than we do."

"Yep," David agreed. "Veer off. We'll make it
look like we're just going to walk past the town."

"Which way?"

"Toward the bakery. Maybe we get lucky, pick
up some food."

We veered. No chatter now. No singing.

Fight or flee. The fundamental decision made
by all aware life-forms. Some always flee. None always fights.

There is something about that moment when
you decide to run away. The recognition that you

are in danger. That the danger is too great to face. Or that at least it represents too great a risk for too little payoff.

In that moment you become prey. And all the instincts of prey come rushing up from the deep brain. Fear. And worse, growing, accelerating fear.

We walked. Falsely casual. Walked and stumbled. Legs simultaneously stiff and rubbery.

A shout. High-pitched, almost girlish. Coming from the slave column.

"They're after us," David grated. "Three guys on horses."

"We take them, that leaves three with the column back there," Christopher said in a rush.

"They're on horseback," David said. "Doubtful we can take them. Definitely can't outrun them."

The horses were in full gallop now. No time to think. Only time to act. Keep moving. Cling to a foolish hope that it wasn't us they were after, or maybe they were just coming to check on us, or maybe they wanted to talk about this weather we've been having.

I tried to control my breathing, take deep, steady breaths. Panic comes when the heart is hammering madly and there's no air to be had, when breathing stops and the blood is crying for oxygen and . . .

I could hear the hooves pounding. The weird, falsetto whoops of the three black-and-silver warriors.

They were too fast. Impossibly fast. They seemed to blow across the desolate landscape like the first fresh assault of a storm.

"Stop. Wait," David said.

"Smile," April advised.

Sure enough, she was smiling.

They were big men, all three. Big men on big horses, all made larger by the armor that encased their chests and shoulders, left their legs bare but for tall, laced boots.

"Go for the legs. If we have to fight, hack their legs," David said.

They were going to run us down, not even stop, just run right over us.

"The horses," I heard myself muttering. "Jesus, look at them."

They were horses, like any other horses, except that each leg split at the knee into two distinct legs and two distinct hooves. Each horse had eight legs.

"Eight-legged horses. Man, what's holding up the leprechauns on unicorns? Don't run," Christopher said. "They're just trying to scare us. And doing a pretty good job."

"They haven't drawn weapons," David said.

Rushing straight at us. My feet were frozen in place. Fight the panic.

A spotted gray horse sideswiped me. Like a full-back hit to the chest. I spun, went down. Felt dirt in my mouth. Curled up in a ball. The hooves!

They were past, turning back at a more placid pace. I uncurled, stood up, shaky, spitting grass and gravel out of my mouth.

Two of the three warriors laughed at us. Weird, tinny laughs. The third, an Asian man as huge as the two massive Norsemen with him, signaled them to shut up.

The Asian rode back to us at a slow walk. Too many hooves crushed too many prints into the dirt and grass.

"Where are you bound, travelers? Have you lost your way? The city gate lies back that way." He pointed helpfully. He sounded like an even higher-pitched Mike Tyson.

April put on her patented "talking to possible psychotics" smile. "We are traveling minstrels. We are lost, but we decided against going into town."

The Asian smiled a slow, mean smile. "Most decide thus," he said. "And yet, many enter. You may leave, my lady. She has no orders for you. You may go or come, as you choose. But these three will certainly enter the city."

I looked up from my fascination with the eight-legged horse and noticed the polished brass oval that rested directly over the man's breastbone. It was stamped with a symbol.

A knife. Dripping blood. Two diamonds beneath it.

"The thing is, we don't have any money for a room or whatever," Christopher said.

"No need of money in Her city," the Asian said. "Food, wine, shelter, all are free to any true man who enters."

"And if we still prefer not to enter?" David asked.

The Asian jerked a brief grin. "You will not make that mistake." He shrugged. "You may walk in freely, or you can be tied, yoked, and whipped through the gates."

For a moment the issue hung in doubt. But not very much doubt. The man on the horse weighed two hundred and fifty pounds, minimum. He was armored and atop a very fast horse. We would be left to hack at his knees while he would be hacking at our heads.

A neat, concise little lesson in the advantage enjoyed by a man on horseback.

David, Christopher, April, and I exchanged looks.

Christopher sighed. "Thanks for the invitation, then, dude. Let's all go into town. Par-tay!"

CHAPTER

VII

The town walls may once have been intended to keep dangers out. But that was all changed now.

The guards faced inward. The inner base of the wall was bordered by a moat, maybe twenty feet wide, badly constructed but effective. Within the moat was an ooze of green-black water, tangled weeds, mudflats like overturned rafts. As I watched, one of those mudflats moved, slid into the water, green scale slithering after green scale.

Once inside, the path to the gate became a causeway. It narrowed to a width that would allow no more than two people abreast.

At both ends of the causeway was a guardhouse, a squat rock building with large, open windows all around. A dozen men, all large, all armored like the Asian, lounged and drank and looked mean.

We came in just steps ahead of the column of men and . . . and whatever. . . . The guards jeered us all, and all in nearly identical high-pitched voices.

"They look tough, but, man, they sound like a bunch of 'N Sync fans," Christopher said.

"Maybe some kind of interbred thing, you know, not entirely human, despite what they look like," David suggested.

"They're eunuchs," I said.

"They're what?" Christopher demanded.

"The bloody knife on their breastplates? The jewels? It's a symbol. They're eunuchs. Castrated males."

"Oh, jeez, don't say that word."

"They used to do it back in, like, the Renaissance. In Italy, maybe. They'd take young boys before they hit puberty, castrate them. So they could sing soprano in the church choir."

We kept walking, trying to get across the causeway as fast as possible. It was hard not to be nervous, thinking that a wrong step would land you with the alligators below.

Just over the causeway, barely back onto solid ground, two soprano guardsmen stepped up, and in a bored, indifferent tone, demanded our weapons.

"I'm not giving up my sword," David said. "This is Galahad's sword."

A backhanded swipe caught him unprepared, full in the face. He staggered back onto the causeway. He reached for the hilt of his sword.

I reached for my weapon. No other choice. Had to stand with David, man, we had to stand together. Happened too fast. I drew.

Suddenly the causeway moved. It retracted, back toward the gate. A four-foot gap opened up between David and me. The movement knocked David off his feet altogether. He was on his knees, guards rushing up behind him across the causeway, swords drawn.

Nothing I could do for him. Too far to reach. Guards closing around me and Christopher now.

The first man to reach David kicked him hard in his chest. The second pinioned his sword arm. The causeway slid back toward us, allowing them to drag David off onto solid ground.

It had all happened very fast. The eunuchs were good. Something to remember.

"You want your sword?" A man built like an SUV slammed his fist into the side of David's head. "You want your sword? I will let you keep your sword. Only give me your jewels and I will let you keep your sword."

The other guards all laughed uproariously at this, a chorus of massive, threatening schoolgirls.

He must have been a captain of the guards. Some rules still hold true in Everworld: Men still laughed too loudly at a boss's joke.

The monster of a man grabbed David's left ankle, used his foot to hold the other ankle down, and spread David like a turkey wishbone.

He drew a long, curved knife.

"You want your sword? Tell me now and you may join us."

"Take the sword," David grunted.

The captain let David go. David couldn't stand up. I ran to him, along with April. Helped him to his feet.

The captain leaned over and picked up Galahad's sword.

"Aaahh!" he cried out, a hysterical whinny.

He dropped the sword and held up his hand, shocked. The man's palm was livid red. Blisters were swelling, bubbling the skin.

"Enchantment!" the captain whimpered. He gave David a hard look. A harder look at the sword lying on the ground.

I saw David make the instant calculation to pretend that all this was expected. It was not. I had handled Galahad's sword and not been burned. Christopher as well.

"My sword doesn't like you," David said evenly.

"This is witchcraft." The man looked uncertain.

"I give you my word of honor that I will not raise this sword against any man within this city," David said.

"Or woman," I interjected quickly.

"Or woman," David agreed.

The guard captain squared his shoulders, huffed and puffed out his footlocker chest. "She will not fear your sword. Your witchery will not harm Her." All that in a loud voice calculated to carry to his men. He leaned into David. "If you try to escape, I will cut you myself. How you will howl! And I will cook your jewels with wine and herbs."

They gave a perfunctory search to April's backpack, found nothing troubling, and kicked Christopher in the rear end for good measure.

We had been dismissed. We didn't wait around for the man to change his mind.

"What's with 'jewels'?" Christopher wondered. "Does he mean the jewels in the sword handle?"

"Christopher? Think," I said.

"Oh."

"Exactly."

Chapter VIII

"Well, we still have one sword," David said. "That has to help."

Christopher laughed. "Help us do what? Get across the moat? Over the walls? Around those Big-Gulp–sized nancy boys?" He spread his hands wide, indicating the streets and square around us. "Look at this place, Napoleon. It's an all-male freak show. This many guys can't bust out, and you figure one sword will turn it all around?"

He was right. It was all-male. Or nearly. But not all human, not by a long shot.

Humans there were, in sizes ranging from World Wrestling Federation on down to men's gymnastics. Skin colors from espresso to skim milk. Eyes as pale as a winter's sky or as dark as coals. Red hair, black hair, blond hair, brown, and sandy, long, short, and weird.

But not a gray hair. Not a bald pate.

The human men were all fairly young. There might have been a few over thirty. But not many. And, whether they were big or small, black, white, or Asian, they were strong, healthy specimens of humanity.

Too healthy. Too healthy for a society that from all outward appearances was stuck around the year 1000, give or take a handful of centuries. There were too many mouths full of too many teeth. Too much clear skin. Too many straight legs, too many strong arms.

We'd stayed two nights with the sorts of people you'd expect to find in this culture. These were not those people.

Humans seemed to make up about seventy percent of the population. The next largest group, maybe another twenty percent of the total, were dwarfs. *Not* small humans, dwarfs.

They were recognizably a different species: oversized heads, short legs, massive shoulders and barrel chests, elongated faces. Big, rough hands and large feet. They managed to be small in the complete picture and yet, somehow, large in all the details.

They did not wear comical coned hats and pointed shoes. They wore supple body armor, bright chain-mail shirts that hung down to just above their knees, brown leather breeches, and wide leather belts draped over their shoulders like Miss America sashes.

You didn't see them and think you could push them around. There was something pit-bullish about them. Small, yes. Harmless, no.

The remaining ten percent included half a dozen species: thin, faintly green-skinned, brilliantly green-eyed, Calista-Flockhart–thin elves; a handful of glum, almost comic, Groucho-walking Coo-Hatch aliens; an occasional troll; something so hairy we couldn't be sure what it was; something dark and small and stooped that clung to the shadows and was visible mostly from the glitter of sharp teeth; and, clop-clopping from here to there, centaurs.

We paused, well away from the gate, away from the moat, in a narrow square hemmed by overhanging three-story buildings.

Christopher had a satisfied look on his face. "Well, here we are: the home office of weird. Those are centaurs. Half-horse, half-man cen-freaking-taurs. I'm telling you, leprechauns cannot be far off. If we had a box of Lucky Charms, man, they'd be on us."

"All male," I said. "All fairly young. I've seen about three females."

"Are you saying these guys just felt like hanging out here in the middle of nowhere?"

April said, "No. It's pretty obvious something's wrong. These guys are all scared."

David nodded. "Like a dentist's waiting room. Scared people. They're prisoners, but not starving. The guy said they had free food. So let's get some. Eat first, figure this stuff out after."

"Elves. We are walking around in the street with elves," Christopher said.

I wasn't sure if he was impressed or amused or indignant.

Another time I would have found it all fascinating. We were taking a walk through a town that might have been lifted directly out of medieval Europe. Pigs and chickens ran in the streets. The buildings leaned so far out over the streets that the early evening sky was reduced to an irregular ribbon of darkest blue. The stench of animal droppings, human droppings, pee, beer, sweat, and goats was powerful but not overwhelming.

It was like a walk through history. Only from time to time I would brush past the swift, fleeting, disturbingly beautiful form of an elf.

We followed the streets, not finding anything to eat or drink. I found I was looking for neon signs. A twenty-first-century, urban American, I was looking for a sign that advertised food. Golden arches, perhaps. Then it occurred to me to try a simpler method.

"I smell food," I said.

"I smell former food," Christopher replied. "I smell stuff I don't want to think about."

We turned a corner. The intersections tended not to be squared off. Geometry, or at least city planning, was at best an approximate science here.

Around the corner I lost the smell of food. And saw something that drove thoughts of food out of my head.

Half a dozen men were moving slowly down the street toward us. An ox cart slogged placidly behind them. The men were reaching up with long poles, curved into blunt scythes at the end.

Reaching up and scraping something from the fronts of buildings that seemed to have been slammed or buckled inward.

The something they were scraping hung in gray tatters and made a soft, wet splat as it was dislodged and hit the cobblestones.

And a softer splat as they slung it into the ox cart.

Something large had walked down this street, pushing in shutters and cracking walls. And leaving in its wake a trail of putrid, gray, decomposed flesh.

CHAPTER
IX

It was true that in this town, this town whose
only name seemed to be "Her City," they fed
you, housed you, and gave you all the ale or wine
or mead or mare's milk or, if you insisted, water,
you could want.

We found an inn far from the trail of dead
flesh. It was on the river side of town.

On that side the town rested atop a bluff. The
outer wall of the city ran along the base of the
bluff, just back from the water's edge. The result
was a sort of no-man's land: buildings up high, a
scrub-grown cliff, a belt of cleared land, the wall
itself, and beyond the wall, out of sight, the river.

The eunuchs patrolled the belt of open land.
Any attempt to escape in that direction would
require a descent down a cliff through thorn-

bushes, evading the patrols, climbing the wall, and then somehow fording the river.

We had no idea of the condition of the river at that point. It might be shallow or deep, lazy or wild. There was a single bridge. We could see the gate leading to it, but not the bridge itself. The gate was guarded and flanked by sharp-toothed towers.

Once we found the inn we went up to our room to check it out before dinner. I guess four to a room was about normal. No one offered us a second room and when Christopher hinted, the hint went unnoticed.

The room was not the presidential suite of the Ritz-Carlton. But it wasn't awful, either.

"You know, I hate to say this, but compared to where we've slept lately this looks pretty good," David said.

"No chickens, no goats, no talking pigs," April agreed.

"Hey, let's check the TV and see if they get satellite movies. What was that movie with that killer leprechaun? Bet they show that on every channel."

"You know, you're starting to get a little fixated on leprechauns," David said.

"I'm just being prepared," Christopher said.

"Dragons, trolls, unicorns, gods, giant wolves, it's just a matter of time."

The room was furnished with two large, sagging, no-doubt flea-ridden beds. Four-posters with shabby coverlets and ratty feather quilts. The sheet had apparently not made its way to this corner of Everworld just yet.

"April and I will take this one," Christopher announced.

"David, I'll need to borrow the sword," she said without missing a beat.

David pushed open the shutters on the window. They'd been closed a long time, judging by the fact that he had to climb on a chair and kick repeatedly to work the rusted hinges. We crowded around to see the view.

We were perched right above the bluff. The wall went down three stories, then melded almost unnoticeably into cliff face. We could see over the outer wall of the city, but still could not see the water.

We did, however, have a splendid view of the triangular mountain that loomed up from beyond the river. Nearness did not improve the mountain's appearance. It was still a monstrous, half-overgrown slag heap with a machete-cut scar down its face.

And now we could see the cave.

It was nothing but a blank, black hole in the rock. Just a cave. Just a hole perhaps forty feet high and somewhat less wide.

And yet I felt my pulse quicken. Felt the tingling of the tiny hairs up and down the length of my spine. And I heard the sudden silence that stilled even Christopher's voice.

There was a pathway, just barely visible in the light of the rising moon, a serpentine path leading down from the cave. I couldn't see it join with the far side of the bridge over the river, couldn't prove that the pathway led directly from that cave to this town, but in the absence of definitive facts you can infer from your own experience.

Or maybe you can just know because something down in the deep recesses of your animal brain, something buried way beneath all the layers of reason and rationalization and denial and skepticism, something down there just knows danger.

That, too, is a fact: that we are members of an animal species that somehow survived for a million years before the first demand for evidence.

"Not liking that," Christopher muttered. "Not liking that at all."

"Nothing to be afraid of," April said. "Just a big hole in the ground, right, Jalil?"

I didn't say anything. Just a big hole in the ground. And a pathway. And flesh hanging from third-floor windowsills. And a lot of scared men guarded by eunuchs in a town they called "Hers."

We went downstairs to the dining room. There was a long plank table down the center of the room and several smaller tables in the dark corners. Three men sat together, hunched over their food at one end of the plank table. A lone dwarf sat by himself near the fire, nursing a tankard the size of his own head.

The two men facing us looked up as we came down. Shot quick, appreciative looks at April, then looked away. The dwarf took a long swallow and stared into his beer.

"So, I guess we missed happy hour," Christopher joked. "Not exactly Applebee's on all-you-can-eat shrimp night, is it?"

"There's an empty table over there." David pointed.

"No, we should mingle," I said. "We need some clue as to what's going on around here."

We sat at the long plank table, leaving a gap between ourselves and the three men. We didn't want to seem too pushy.

A waitress, an old woman with straggly gray

hair and fat arms, put food down in front of us. Steaming lentils, half a dozen greasy sausages, a bowl of what might have been cottage cheese, some honeyed parsnips, and a loaf of crusty white bread.

"Drink?" she asked.

"What are the choices?"

The crone gave us a hard look, like maybe we thought we were too good for the establishment. "There's beer, wine, bark tea, and fermented mare's milk."

"Beer," Christopher said quickly.

David pursed his lips, a strangely feminine expression of disapproval. "Tea for me. Make sure the water has been boiled."

April and I went along with David. And then we attacked the food. I mean attacked. The bread disappeared in seconds, ripped apart like the only rabbit at a coyote convention.

I wolfed the lentils. Followed by sausage. I had serious doubts about the sausage but it had been very well cooked and I was craving protein. April finished my parsnips.

"This tea tastes like hot root beer," April said.

Christopher smacked his lips. "This beer tastes like beer. Not too late to change your order. Ma'am! Waitress! More beer, please."

She brought a new tankard and Christopher grinned and said, "That old lady is the Saint Pauli Girl after a lifetime of hard drinking."

"I wonder if this town has a name?" I said, deliberately pitching my voice to be overheard. "Everyone just calls it 'Her City.' Has to have a name."

Nothing. The three men signaled the old woman for refills. They were well on their way to being drunk.

"I mean, who is this 'Her'?"

"Shut up, you damned fool."

I looked at the man who'd spoken. He had dark hair, very pale skin, and serious gray eyes. He was a handsome man. Like most of the men in the town.

"Why? We can't even ask who 'She' is?"

"You may find out soon enough. As may we all, may the Daghdha preserve us."

He looked pointedly away. But his companion, a red-haired man with the swollen, veined nose and ruddy cheeks of the confirmed drinker, was not as circumspect. Or as sober.

"Lost, then, are you? Poor wayfarers dragged here against your will and all at sea?"

"Pretty much," David confirmed.

"Have you not noticed this is a city of men, then?"

"We had noticed that."

"Have you not seen the dark black tunnel, that gateway to the nether regions, then?"

"We've seen that, too," David allowed. "Does it lead somewhere?"

The red-faced man gaped, then exploded in laughter. "Yes, it does indeed lead somewhere. Or anywhere. Or everywhere, so they say. A man who travels that road and lives may climb back up to any place in Everworld, or in the Old World itself."

Four heads jerked in unison. We stared as April lowered her voice, trying unsuccessfully to conceal her eagerness. "The Old World? Are you saying that you can reach the Old World through that tunnel?"

"Not at all, lass."

"You just said —"

"I said a man who travels that road and lives. And *lives*, do you see? There's the difficulty, then." He leaned forward and his bluff, hearty demeanor evaporated. "No man travels that path and lives. Fear itself will kill him. I know. I have seen my own brother — as brave a man as ever was, a warrior of the Fianna, as are we all, protectors of the High Kings, and all good men and true — seen him scream and cry like a baby and tear at his own eyes with his hands like claws, like the claws of an eagle, so that the blood ran and still he screamed, so terrible was the fear.

"Aye," he continued, and went back to his beer. "To live, that's the trick."

CHAPTER

X

Back in our room. Window shuttered. Candle flickering, casting weird, wild shadows around the room.

We were shaken. Talking too much, too fast. No one thinking about opening the window for a late-night view of the cave.

Christopher said, "He was just yanking our chains, man. Telling ghost stories for the rubes. Like at camp where they start in with the new kids and all that chainsaw massacre, man-with-a-hook b.s."

"He seemed —" April began.

"That's all it was, man."

"— like he believed what he was saying."

"Which doesn't make it true," I pointed out. "Superstitious people and —"

"But what if he's right? You know, about being able to get back to the real world? Back home?"

David said, "You forget: You are back home. There's an April back there right now, in class, or asleep, or whatever. So we show up and we're an extra set of us?"

April erupted. "It's just sick with you, David. You don't want to go home — well, I do. We all do. All but you, you sick —"

"I'm just saying maybe it's —"

"Hey, it's probably all bull, but we don't exactly have a better plan, and maybe it'll work," Christopher said. "I mean, even if David's right, so there's two of me, what do I care as long as neither of me is here?"

"No one is going home without Senna; we agreed on that," David said.

"Agreed, hell!" Christopher snapped. "Senna belongs in this big, open-air nuthouse."

David slammed his hand against the shutters. "You don't leave one of your own behind."

"She's not one of my anything, man, she's —"

"We'll never find her unless she wants to be found," April said. "And if she wants to be found, we don't want to find her."

"And when Loki does find her? And when he turns her into this gateway and suddenly Loki and Huitzilopoctli and all the rest of these things start spilling out into the real world?"

April threw up her hands. "We can't stop them, David. Get a grip on reality. It's a miracle we're alive. We're lost and pathetic and filthy and wandering around like morons — we . . . I mean, what do you think is going to happen, David? You're going to catch up with Senna and the two of you will be Batman and Batgirl and go off and save Everworld? Are you that deluded?"

"David just really wants a piece of that," Christopher sneered. "Not enough women in the world, no, G.I. freaking Joe here, with his magic sword, has to have that particular piece."

"Shut up, Christopher, you're not helping," April snapped.

At which point Christopher used a harsh word, and April threw it back in his face, slightly modified.

David held up his hands, palms out. "Look, obviously we're all a little worked up. We're tired. We're creeped out. Let's get some sleep. Nothing is going to be decided now, with us all slamming one another. I'll take first watch."

April ran her hand back through her red hair and shook her head. "I shouldn't have eaten that sausage, but I was so hungry. Meat makes me crazy. Look, let's just . . . look, we'll find out if other people say the same thing. About that tunnel leading to the real world. That's all I'm saying. We find out, right? We keep an open mind."

She sighed. "Man, I'd trade a year of my life for a hot shower."

Everyone fell silent at once. Then David looked at me. "What, you have nothing to say, Jalil? You're just above it all?"

"I agree with April."

"About me being a jerk?"

"About the shower."

Christopher laughed a little. April just looked haunted. Maybe it was the weird light, but it seemed to me her eyes were drawn again and again to the shuttered window. To the tunnel that lay in that direction.

Home. Out of Everworld. We all wanted that. Didn't we?

April and I shared one bed, David and Christopher the other. I guess that was the "safe" arrangement. Some sort of subterranean interpersonal politics going on there that I was too tired to try and figure out. Anyway, that's how it worked out. No one undressed. Not a question of modesty, an unspoken acknowledgment that despite the walls and the doors, we felt no safer here than we had in the forest.

I lay there on my back, carefully not thinking about the fact that I could feel April's body warmth, and looking up at the darkness. Sleep. Sleep would take us all home.

Did I want that? April was desperate to escape Everworld. David just as desperate — though less honest — about wanting to stay. It wasn't just that he was still under Senna's spell. It was the sword at his side and the adrenaline pumping in his veins.

And me? I always knew what I wanted. But not at this moment.

I was in the land of madness. But here the madness was all without. When sleep came I would return to the land where madness was within me.

"Nice choice," I whispered.

Why me, Senna? Why drag me into this?

Don't think about that, Jalil. Just sleep. Go home to the real world. Sleep.

I woke and found myself at my part-time job, Boston Market. I reached with the unconscious ease of long practice to snag a freshly cooked chicken with my tongs. I laid the knife's edge on the breastbone, ready to split it.

I looked down and saw Senna's head growing from the empty hole of the chicken's neck.

CHAPTER
XI

I was asleep. I realized that. Asleep both here and there. I'd crossed over into a nightmare. Or maybe I'd brought the nightmare with me, I don't know.

Senna's head tried to speak. Her mouth moved but no sound came out.

"I need a quarter white!" the assistant manager yelled. "Come on, Jalil, quarter white."

Only now the assistant manager was a Hetwan. The round head with the two huge insect eyes; the three grasping claws that ringed the almost-human mouth and seemed to be in an eternal search for food to snatch from the air; the folded-back wings.

"What is it with you and that chicken, Jalil? Cut her. Cut her open. Customers are waiting," the Hetwan said. "Ka Anor is waiting."

No. Couldn't. She was laughing at me. Senna now. I leaned into the knife, but it had no effect. The bones wouldn't split.

But my hands, yes, I could cut them off. I could lay my wrist down on the counter, as I was doing, just testing to see if I could, press my hand down, fingers splayed, take the knife and lay the cold steel on the back of my wrist and one quick, sudden movement, no more hand. All gone. How to wash then?

I laughed. Hysterical. Unable to stop.

"Ah-ahhh," I moaned.

Awake. No light in the windows. No sounds in the house. My folks asleep. My two little sisters asleep in the room they shared.

I was home. Real world. I felt the update, the sudden acquisition of understanding, traded information between my two halves. Files merging.

Ah, real-world Jalil, so you worked on that Web site with Tony and Dawes.

Yes, Everworld Jalil, we almost have it up and running, and I see you've been busy as well, what with being trapped by eunuchs in some kind of city of the damned.

Two became one in mind and memory at least. My body, the physical other me, remained asleep in Everworld.

I rolled out of bed. Had to pee. Rubbed sleep

from my eyes and tried to shake off the creepy effect of the nightmare. I didn't try and make sense of the dream. Dreams were just brain farts. They didn't mean anything except as a distorted catalog of whatever happened to have bothered you during the day.

I stood up, turned around, and arranged my three pillows in precise formation. Two side by side, one on top, precisely centered.

I went to the bathroom, moving as quietly as I could. Banged my toe on the door, cursed under my breath, fumbled my way to the bathroom.

I slipped inside before flicking on the light. The toilet lid was up. I closed it. Then opened it again. Couldn't start without the toilet lid having been closed.

I checked behind the shower curtain, as I always did.

Senna was there.

I took three quick breaths, but none reached my lungs. Suddenly the bathroom walls pushed out and away in all directions. Not my bathroom anymore. There were tall tables with individual sinks. Racks of test tubes. Locked glass-front cabinets full of white plastic bottles, each neatly labeled.

The chem lab at school.

Dark. Fluorescents off, and the only light was

what came filtered through the ancient venetian blinds. I heard the sounds of end-of-school-day high spirits from outside.

I stood at the sink and washed my hands.

And again.

And again.

And began to cry and rage at myself, despising myself, hating the quirk of brain that controlled me this way.

Then, a sound. In the room.

No, no, no, no.

Turned and looked over my shoulder. A girl I knew slightly from one of my classes. She was thin but not extraordinarily so. Tall but not very. Pretty rather than beautiful. She wore a long, wrap-around skirt. A sheer blouse, white cotton, two buttons open.

She had eyes as gray as the zinc tabletops in the lab. She had an odd name: Senna.

"I was just . . ." I started to say. But just what? Just been washing my hands over and over while I called myself terrible things?

"Your name is Jalil," she said.

I nodded.

She moved closer. Watched me. Studied me. Considered me. Was I useful? That was the question on her face, in her eyes. Not, "Is he crazy?" Just, "Will he do?"

She stopped, ten feet away. I still held my hands up, awkward, dripping wet, like a surgeon scrubbing for an operation. I stared at her. Wanted to go back to the sink, felt the urge so badly, as strong as ever in my life, a burning need more ferocious than any imaginable hunger.

She nodded. Decision made.

"I can help you," she said.

No point denying anything, she knew. The first person ever to know besides me. "No. No one can help."

"Touch me," she said.

She made no further move toward me. Just waited. From outside I heard someone yell, "Okay, now you're dead," but playfully.

I took a step. Stopped. "Look, it's called obsessive-compulsive, okay? It's embarrassing, I'm humiliated, okay? But it's just this thing, this . . ."

"Touch me, Jalil."

Another step. No! This was insane, absurd. She was playing with me, mocking me.

Step. Step.

So close now. Another step and I'd be able to reach out and touch her. She'd been only pretty, but now she was overwhelming. Not beautiful, overwhelming. I wanted to touch her. To hold her. Kiss.

"I can help you, Jalil."

Another step.

"It's an act of faith, Jalil."

That stopped me like a slap in the face. "I don't do faith."

"You must have faith in something."

I shook my head. "If you have knowledge, you don't need faith." Something I'd said before.

She cocked her head, amused. "Ah. One of those. You want proof."

I nodded, uncertain. I still wanted to touch her. Wanted her to insist that I touch her. Wanted.

She was going to walk away. No. She wasn't. Why?

"I'll make a deal with you, Jalil. A trade. A step for a step."

She moved toward me. So close now.

I stepped.

Inches. I could feel her breath against my face. I still held my hands, my dirty, dirty hands up, waiting to be washed again.

"I will take the need from you," she whispered. "I can give you peace. I can release you. Only touch me."

"Where?"

She smiled.

I reached out my hand, and as I reached I trembled, and as I reached I fought within myself, told myself it was all stupid, told myself it was okay, I was merely putting her claim to the test.

My fingers met resistance.

And oh . . . oh, it was gone. Gone. The need, all gone. The nagging, insane voice that urged me always, controlled me, that never-silenced, never-satisfied voice was gone.

Madness. The touch had cured me. Impossible! All in my head, some placebo effect of course, a temporary thing. The distraction of this girl, this creature whose flesh felt so cold.

Peace. Silence within me. Peace.

"What do you want?" I asked her.

"A cynic as well as a rationalist?" she said, mocking me openly now. "What do I want? To own you, Jalil. To know that if I ever need you, you will be mine to use."

"No," I said, but not firmly.

"Oh, I think yes. It must be very painful for you, smart, sensible, in control as you are, to be so out of control, to have that nasty little demon in your head telling you what to do. Much worse for you than it would be for most people. But I can give you peace."

I pulled my hand away. Broke the connection.

I saw the look of surprise, the swift passage of rage, coming and going like a gust of wind. She regained control of her emotions.

As I lost control. The obsession was alive in my head once again. The nagging, insistent voice was back, all the louder after the brief silence.

"You think I'm weak, Senna," I managed to say. "You think I'm weak because I can't control this part of myself. You're wrong. My own brain messes with me, but I am still who I am."

"I wonder," she said, then turned and walked away.

I woke. This time for real. My pillow was damp. Sheets whipped every which way.

I took a shaky breath. A dream inside a dream. But a memory, too. Just as it had happened. How long ago now? Six, seven months? I should remember the day when for one moment I was free.

Now I was in my room, in my world, with both sets of memories, both lives temporarily united.

I got out of bed. Had to pee. Had to wash my hands.

CHAPTER
XII

"Get up, something's happening," David hissed.

I opened my eyes. April was moving beside me. Rolling away from me. I felt lingering warmth — and numbness — where her elbow had crossed my left arm.

"What is it?" I asked. Was this another dream? No. No. I'd woken up finally. I had been conscious over there.

And now I was here again. Conscious.

The room was dark. Still night. And I sensed it was not very late, that I had not been asleep for very long.

I heard a raucous, feminine voice from outside. Far off, but loud enough to be heard. I got up. Christopher was just wiping the sleep from his eyes and complaining.

April said, "What's going on?"

"Don't know," David said. "Listen."

We strained to hear. Looking at one another or at nothing and listening.

The raucous voice cried out, "Who shall it be, oh, who shall it be, that serves the needs of the Terror Queen?"

And then the voice laughed, wonderfully amused by her own little ditty.

"Let's open the shutters," I said. I walked over and pushed them open, cautiously. I peeked through the crack. The moon was up. A faint, unclean glow illuminated the rock face of the mountain. The cave was a pit of black. Something moving in front of it. Coming out of it, or passing in front of it, impossible to tell. Impossible to tell much except that it was too large to be human.

"What now?" Christopher said, exasperated.

"She's coming this way," April said. "Going to cross the bridge."

"You sure it's a 'she'?" I asked. "All the eunuchs around here —"

"It's a 'she,'" April said positively. "Anyway, she called herself the Terror Queen."

"Could be a big, mean transvestite," Christopher said. "Of course, she'd have to be a big, mean, transvestite Loch Ness monster to really stand out in a crowd around here."

Again the big voice chortled. "Ah, they welcome me. Do you want me so badly, then, that
you play coy? Three, is it? And the useless
fourth?"

I had the odd feeling she was talking to us.
Couldn't be. She couldn't see us from so far away,
through a dark window.

The Queen, or whatever she was, went temporarily out of sight beneath the line of the walls.

From the streets outside there came noises.
Men's voices. Scared.

"She's coming this way!"

"You fool, don't cry out!"

Scuffling sounds. Fighting. Cries of anger, fear.

The door burst in. It was the red-faced man
who'd called himself a warrior of the Fianna.
With him was the old woman who'd served our
food.

"You damned fools!" The man rushed for the
window and slammed it shut. "Why not just call
out to Her, you silly twits? You've drawn Her to
this house."

"What is this?" David demanded.

"My house to be all torn apart," the crone
cried, wringing her arthritic fingers.

"Hide yourselves, if you can," the Fiannan
said. He shot a look at April. "And for all love,

keep the girl from her. She's a beauty, and hell will brook no competition."

He slammed from the room, yelling, "Run, everyone out, the bloody fools have drawn her here!" The crone went with him, still moaning about her house.

"I didn't think pagans believed in hell," April said. "But anything they call hell has got to be bad enough. Let's get out of here."

"Got that right," Christopher said.

We piled out of the room. David ran, buckling on his sword as he went. We clattered down the stairs. Rushed through the dining room.

Into the street. No one in sight but a brief glimpse of two men disappearing around the corner.

"Follow them," David said, and off we went.

It was dark in the narrow streets. The moonlight didn't reach down this far. The cobblestones were uneven. We tripped. Reached a corner and could not even tell how many streets led away from it, or in what directions.

"Ow. Watch it. Here, there's a low wall or something."

"Okay, this way. There's a street."

We started moving again, but slowly. Keeping in touch by staying huddled together.

"It's lighter up ahead," I said.

"Yeah. Let's go that way."

We trotted, hand in hand, hand on belt. David had been carrying his sword at the ready but he sheathed it now. Too much danger of an accident.

Ahead, silvery moonlight turned buildings gray like an old black-and-white photograph. We emerged from the narrow street into a more open place, a sort of trapezoidal public square. There was even a fountain in the middle. It dribbled water from the mouths of stylized lions.

And then, a noise behind us. From the very street we'd just left, I spun around and saw her.

She glowed in the moonlight. But also from some deeper, inner light. She was huge, of course, maybe twice the height of a man, but beautiful beyond any beauty I'd ever imagined.

I saw Her only in profile. A lustrous blue-green eye. Cascading black hair. Skin so pale and translucent she might have been formed of the early-morning sunlight. She was perfectly formed in every aspect. A long leg, bared by the slit in her flimsy, breeze-tossed, barely seen dress. A firm, inviting breast. Taut, smooth flesh. Perfect, down to the shape of her ear, the fingers of her hand.

I could not look away. I knew in some rational part of my mind that no one woman could ever be that perfect, that it was absurd to talk of perfect beauty when there are a million different beauties. I knew my reaction was distorted. That some spell . . .

And yet, I found myself walking toward her, unable to do otherwise. *So* beautiful.

"Ah, there you are," she said. "Do you find me beautiful? Do you lust for me? I will test your ardor."

She turned to face me.

I screamed.

CHAPTER
XIII

I screamed and screamed and screamed.

I heard my own cries, heard the animal terror of my friends, their jibbering, babbling cries of horror.

Was I on my knees? *Stand up. Run! Run, Jalil.*

But I could not stop screaming. A sound came from me that I could not make. Couldn't. Could I? That hideous, nightmare howl? Was that from me?

The spun-gossamer dress that had left me helpless with desire for her right side now revealed the vile detail of her left side.

She was dead. She was death itself.

Her flesh was the color of raw concrete. Gray. Ash. But with spots of color like bruises: yellow and green and purple.

Her eye was an empty socket, dark as the cave she'd come from. The left side of her nose was eaten away, gnawed down to the cartilage. There was a rip in her cheek, revealing the rotting, gumless teeth in her mouth. Her tongue writhed with worms that lived within the dead flesh itself.

Her left leg was formed like her right, her left breast like her right, but in a terrible time-lapse photo that showed the awful ravages of death and time. The worms ate at her, poked in and out of her skin. Maggots formed foul pockets of feverish activity within her very flesh.

Folds of skin hung loose where she had scraped through the narrow streets.

Down the whole length of her body, living, vibrant, luscious flesh met decayed, decomposed, worm-eaten filth. The bright eye was mirrored by the empty socket. The full red lips found their counterpart in maggot-chewed shreds. The hair was parted neatly down the middle, movie-star tresses on one side, and on the other a scraped, skeletal pate boasting only a few brittle strands.

As her beauty had been too bewitching, now her ugliness reached too deep, destroyed all attempts to come to grips with it, and squeezed unfiltered terror from my brain.

And yet here was the true mental destruction

of this monster: The desire never lessened. Even as I screamed and moaned in fear, I craved and wanted and lusted.

"I usually enjoy more of a chase," she said, pouting just a little. "You've made it almost too easy. As for you —" She looked at April and shook her head, letting fall wet chunks of her own flesh. "I wonder how pretty you'll be after I've had you flayed."

"What do you want?" April cried.

I was shocked. How could she speak? How could she form words?

I tore my eyes from the monster. Looked at April. Felt the horror lessen, just the smallest bit. April was horrified, sickened, but not paralyzed as I had been, as Christopher and David were.

Of course. The horror was for men. The magic was directed. Aimed.

"What do I want?" The creature pretended to consider. "I want to lie with these three. I want them to pleasure me through the long, cold night. And when they have screamed and cried and obeyed my every whim, I will add their voices to the chorus of agony that lulls me to sleep each night."

A harem, I thought. *Of course. What else is guarded by eunuchs?* The town was a harem. Men chosen and kept penned in to cater to the depraved needs of the monster.

The creature laughed from a mouth that was at once inviting and repellant. "How have you come to spend time in my city and not know my needs? Am I not a woman? Do I not need a gentle embrace? A soft touch?"

"If you're . . . if you're a woman . . ." April said, "you must have —"

"Must?!" the beast roared in sudden rage. "Must?" She formed a fist with her dead left hand. Squeezed it tight till the flesh parted and bony knuckles poked through. "I am Hel! Ruler of Nifleheim! Daughter of Loki! No mortal tells me I *must*!"

She straightened. "Bring these four. They will amuse me."

Only then did I realize we were surrounded. Silent, unnoticed, a dozen eunuch guards had come up behind us. They stood ready, swords drawn. They wore strange helmets, bright steel that enclosed their heads. A slit visor was shadowed by a bill almost like a baseball cap.

They could see us. But they could not, without straining their necks, see the face of Hel. No one was going to strain to see that.

I looked down. Could not avoid seeing Hel's legs, feet, the dropped chunks of gray-bruised flesh. I felt the horror still. But no longer the paralysis. No longer the uncontrollable need to scream and yet moan with desire.

"Her face," I said in a shaken whisper to the others. "Look away from her face."

We kept our eyes down. The madness passed. A bit, at least. But there was no ounce of energy or will to resist in any of us. The madness faded. The memory lingered. We followed Hel as she strode purposefully through the streets, entertaining herself by smashing a window here and kicking a doorway there, but always drawing us in her wake, through the hushed, relieved city.

To the mountain. To the cave. To the place where Hel, daughter of Loki, ruled.

CHAPTER
XIV

Through the town. Across the bridge. It was a covered, enclosed bridge. No mystery as to why. Men passing this way would gladly have thrown themselves into the water.

"What are we gonna do, man? What are we gonna do?" Christopher asked in a teeth-chattering whisper. "Gotta kill her, man, gotta take her down, I'm not doing *anything* with her, man. No way, no way."

Across the bridge. To emerge on the far side of the river, directly beneath the crushing mass of that slag-heap mountain. The moon was behind the clouds now, providing no light. The darkness was so deep we might have been swimming through ink.

But we could see our way. The dead half of Hel

glowed faintly. Like the fading light of a watch's radium dial.

The pathway was cobblestoned with large, smooth, round stones. It was hard to walk on them. Hard not to trip, especially when you could spare no part of your brain for the task of taking care. We stumbled and tripped and were harshly dragged to our feet by the eunuchs.

Couldn't blame them. Not much. They were doing what they had to do. I tripped hard and landed on my hands and knees. A eunuch stepped forward and yanked me up by my ears.

At that moment the moon came out from behind the clouds. I recognized the face. It was the guard who'd burned his hand trying to take Galahad's sword from David.

He held me close, face-to-face for just a fleeting second, during which time he showed me his burned palm. Then jerked his head toward Hel.

Nothing more. The burned palm. The look toward Hel. And yet I knew it meant something. It was a message.

A message I did not decipher because at that moment April noticed the cobblestones.

"Ohhh!" she wailed. She stopped walking and just stared down.

The cobblestones, thousands of them, all

neatly lined up to form the pathway, were human skulls.

"Keep moving!" burned palm snapped.

We moved, struggling to keep pace with Hel. The evil goddess seemed almost jovial. At one point I could have sworn I heard her singing to herself.

We took a turn and I realized with a shock that we had reached the cave opening. Once inside, all hope was gone. But what was there to do? How was I going to escape? What could I hope to do?

I kept moving. We all kept moving. Should have run. Should have let the guards just cut us down. But then, as though she sensed the moment, Hel turned into profile and knelt down, revealing only the lush beauty that had reduced me to groveling.

How could she intend anything bad? She was so beautiful. So perfect. So indescribably lovely.

She smiled with half her face, showing teeth like perfect pearls. Gave us each in turn a smoldering look from the one wondrously blue-green eye.

I found myself moving toward her.

Hel laughed, amused by her own power and our weakness.

I was inside. In the cave.

Cold. As cold as a December in Chicago. I could see my breath. My skin goose-pimpled.

I had expected darkness. It was dark. But of course the terror of the dark is limited by the powers of one's own imagination. This place, this abode of the Queen of Terror was the product of a mind so diseased, so foul that it far exceeded my own weak powers of imagination. She needed light. And so, light burned from torches placed at intervals along the wall.

The pathway led downward. But no longer over cobblestones of human skulls. Now the pathway was paved with living men.

Living.

They were buried up to the neck, up to the mouth. Heads alone visible. It was row after row of humans, buried so that just their heads emerged from the dirt.

Living, still living, that was it, do you see, they were still alive, alive and moaning or crying or screaming or begging, just heads packed so close together.

They were the cobblestones to be. Near the entrance of the cave living and dead mixed together. Ninety percent dead closest to the entrance. Just a few moaning, delirious creatures, poor creatures, poor desperate murdered men, croaking in the extremity of their agony. Heads flayed. Skull bone already bared.

The living grew more numerous as we progressed. We continued walking, helpless to do anything else, feet landing on scalps, shoes yanking hair, stumbling and kicking defenseless faces.

I heard April's voice. She was praying.

And me? What was I to do? Apologize to the men whose heads I walked on? Apologize? Apologize, sorry? Sorry? What word was there for this?

I was shaking. Teeth not chattering now, but grinding into one another, grinding so that I was sure my teeth would splinter, leaving me to gnaw on the bared nerves.

Impossible! This place could not exist. Home, I wanted to go home, oh please, please, home.

We reached the end of the pathway. Reached the point where a new trench had been dug, ready for the next victims. The next cobblestones.

Ready, perhaps, for us.

CHAPTER
XV

"You're probably expecting to see Garm," Hel said. "Everyone wants to see Hel's hound, but he's at the main entrance to my domain. The official Gnipahelli. I've tried to mate the beast and have a whole litter of Garms, but of course he always eats the pups."

What? What was she saying? She was chatting like we were all off on a picnic together.

"What are your occupations?" Hel asked in a pleasant, conversational tone.

I realized the guards were gone. Left back at the entrance of the cave. But something was following us nevertheless. Dark, flitting, not-quite-visible creatures who slid along the walls, through the shadows.

"I asked a question," Hel said. "What are your

occupations? Are you farmers? Pig tenders? Coopers?"

"We're minstrels," April said.

She was keeping it together better than the rest of us. She faced her own terror, no doubt. But Hel's particular fascination seemed to be males.

"Minstrels, are you?" Hel said. She clapped one live and one dead hand together, like a little girl who's just been told she's going to Baskin-Robbins. "We shall have an entertainment."

"I don't think so," April muttered.

Hel laughed. "Mortal, do you not yet know that I have the power to compel anything? Do you force me to prove what should be very plain for you to see?"

"We'll do a show," Christopher said, keeping his eyes down from Hel's face. "Will you let us go if —"

"You bargain with me? Let you go? Shall I let you go? No one escapes Hel's domain. No, you will do as I say because in so doing you will cling for another few moments to a life without terrible agony. Because it will allow you to hold on to pathetic hope for another short while."

She was right, of course. And utterly confident. Overconfident? I'd have liked to believe that, but that was the very "pathetic hope" she spoke of.

The cave had broadened out to become a vast, seemingly endless underground cavern. It echoed with the sounds of misery. Human voices, no doubt elves and dwarfs and aliens, too.

It was no longer dark so much as misty. Gray. Long fingers of fog or steam floated past. There were open pools of bubbling, steaming glop, maybe mud, maybe something much worse. We might almost have been crossing a brutally cold swamp rather than the stone floor of a cavern.

But this was still clearly Hel's domain. Or at least some edge of it. Creatures came rushing out to her. Dark, misshapen things, twisted mutations of men or dwarfs or elves. At least one looked like an alien species, but who could tell?

They rushed to her and our procession became a sort of weird running business meeting or war council.

"The new tunnel construction has hit a delay, Beautiful Hel. The roof gave in. . . ."

"An emissary from your father awaits in . . ."

"Our forces have strengthened the border with Hades, Oh Most Desirable Queen, but they cry out for reinforcements. . . ."

She gave quick, terse answers to each. A busy executive beset by incompetent subordinates. A general making adjustments to the line of battle.

"Clear the debris, dig out the fools who were

buried, and use their bones to shore up the next section."

"My father's emissary always waits."

"No, I will not reinforce the border with Hades; Hades is not our problem. It is Ahriman we must attack. He is weak! We can seize his domain as easily as we did Ereshkigal's. Persians are no match for my Vikings."

If her pursuing demons had begun handing her memos to sign I would not have been surprised.

With a wave of her dead hand, Hel dismissed her retinue. And now she slowed her pace as we approached what looked like a sort of scale model of Chicago's financial district. Only instead of tall, straight skyscrapers looming above us, they were massive blocks of ice. A dozen to our left, a dozen to our right, forming a parody of a street, an alleyway . . . a graveyard.

The blocks of ice were like chunks of icebergs, white and pale blue and craggy. Craggy except on the side facing the path. There the ice was cut, forming a sheer cliff tilted back at a slight angle.

I gasped, couldn't help myself, when I reached the first ice slab. Within the ice, imprisoned but still alive, was a god dressed like a wealthy Viking. He was handsome, tall, powerfully built.

He was still alive. He still moved. Chest rose

and fell with slow, slow breaths. Mouth opened to form a silent curse. Hand gripped an absent sword, fingers moving slowly, painfully.

"Baldur," Hel said, pausing to admire her captive. "Most beloved of the gods of Asgard. Odin's favorite. And now? All mine. A pity he isn't more cooperative. He is such a fine figure of a god."

She moved on. Ignored a man held on the opposite side, a blue-skinned, multi-armed creature imprisoned in the next block, a woman . . . Passed them by with never a glance. But then she stopped and raised up her lovely living hand to point.

"The prize of my collection."

We looked. It was a god, not a man. Big. Bigger than Loki at his most extreme. Bare arms like tree trunks. Booted legs that could have supported a brachiosaurus.

He had long, wild red-blond hair, a full blond beard, blue eyes, and angry, feral mouth.

In one truck engine fist he gripped a tiny hammer made of scraps of wood nailed together.

Hel must have seen us staring at the hammer. She laughed in glee. Laughed and laughed and pointed at Thor, the still-living god of thunder.

"The hammer is my little joke," Hel said. "My father got the real Mjolnir. Part of the deal."

The Vikings had wondered what became of

their favorite immortal. Here he was, like Baldur, frozen, unable to move except by millimeters.

We left Hel's living sculpture garden. Hel's message of despair had been delivered: I can do this to mighty Thor, just think of what I can do to you.

We had reached a wide space paved with large, flat stones set in a huge circle.

At the center of the circle was a pit fifty feet across. There was no guard rail or curb surrounding the pit.

Horrific cries floated up through the hole. As we passed close by it I carefully avoided looking in. We all did. We had learned our lesson on the road of skulls.

Beyond the pit, set so as to provide a view down into the depths, there was a massive throne. It seemed at first to be made of porous, white stone. But at closer range one could see the bones, glued and fused together, legs and arms, ribs and hands.

Hel mounted the stairs and sat atop her throne. "Now! Entertain me, minstrels."

We blinked stupidly, keeping our gazes averted from her face.

"Oh, pitiful creatures," she sneered. "There. Now you may look at me without collapsing."

I looked up cautiously. A veil had descended

over Hel's face. A fabric like the gossamer that made up her dress. I could still see the contours of her face, the outlines of mouth and eyes, but the effect was lessened.

I could look at her and not scream.

"Sing! Give us a poem! Dance! Quickly, I have much to do. Especially with you, my solemn little man."

She stretched out her living leg, stretched it out toward me, and touched the side of my face with her bare toe.

I cried out and fell back, stunned, shattered. The joy! The ecstasy! Every cell in my brain exploded with the consciousness of pure pleasure.

And then it was gone. I was on my knees. Face wet with my own tears. I would have begged her to touch me again, would have begged on hands and knees, but then she bent low, brought her face close to me.

"Such pleasure you will know, gloomy little man. And such agony. I will tear your mind apart, mortal. I will destroy your very soul, Jalil."

I jerked involuntarily. She knew my name.

She laughed her giddy laugh. "Of course I know you, Jalil, with the uncontrolled demon inside your so-controlled mind. I know each of you. Do you imagine I chose you at random? David,

Christopher, April, all unfortunate visitors from the real world."

"How . . ." David started to ask.

"She reads minds," April said.

"No," I said. "Someone told her."

"Who?" David asked.

I didn't answer. Didn't have to. Only one person could have told this monster who we were, our names, our secrets.

Senna had passed this way. We were on her trail after all.

CHAPTER
XVI

"Don't know why, there's no sun up in the sky, stormy weather," April sang in a shaky voice. "Since my man and I ain't together, keeps rainin' all the time."

Why an old torch song? I don't know. I was just glad she was singing. Just glad to have Hel watching her, listening to her. Anything to keep us from the pit at our backs, or from that hideous road of skulls.

Needed time to think. Needed time to think. Had to be . . . had to be some way . . . to be buried, up to the neck, to lie there starving, fainting from thirst, unable to move, barely able to breathe, my head shredded by passing feet, my . . .

Think, Jalil, don't panic. Push the fear away, think.

What was in the pit? What were those voices crying? Mercy? Was that a cry for mercy I heard?

Forget the pit. There is no pit. Think.

The guard. The one who'd burned his hand on Galahad's sword. He'd let us keep it, why? Because no sword could harm Hel, that had to be it. How did you kill what was already dead?

She had seen the sword. Hel knew David was armed, and she didn't care. Indifferent. That was why the guard had let it go. It didn't matter to Hel. Hel would not punish him for the sword.

And yet . . . there was something else. Something —

"Now dance!" Hel roared.

I jerked into a dance, a wild, stiff-legged, awkward movement. I flailed my arms and Hel laughed gaily. We all danced, around and around, twirling, bumping into one another, weaving.

The sword was different. It had burned the guard's hand, not mine, not Christopher's, only the guard's. Enchantment. Magic. No point fighting it, this was Everworld, the rules were different. *Accept it, Jalil, magic is part of the software of this universe.*

The sword burned any who touched it without permission. And the blade?

I twirled crazily, spinning toward David as all

the while Hel laughed and giggled like the mad
thing she was.

I bumped into David. "The sword," I hissed. "It
can hurt her."

David shook his head and spun away. He
looked back at me, jerked his head toward Hel,
shrugged as if to say, *She's not scared.*

I grabbed him, screw the consequences, we
were dead anyway, and said, "David, damn it,
trust me!"

We separated.

"Who is your fool?" Hel demanded. She peered
at us through the veil. "The one called David? Are
you the fool? No, no, you take yourself far too se-
riously, don't you? The witch warned me about
that."

She pointed a fleshless bone of a finger at
Christopher. "Cavort, fool. Jest. Make me laugh."

"I . . ." He shook his head helplessly. Christopher was shaking, keeping his eyes down, sweat
popping out all over his face. "I could tell a joke."

"Do that."

"Okay, uh, there's a priest, a minister, and a
rabbi, they go into this bar, and —"

"No, no, no, I am not amused. You are very
poor minstrels." Hel looked at David. "Draw your
sword."

Surprised, David drew the sword.

"Now cut off this unfunny fool's ear. His left ear, I believe."

David glared at her and gripped the sword tightly.

"Oh? Are you planning to attack me, mortal? With that?" She pointed at the sword and laughed. "The sword that touches me turns to dust. The arm that wields the sword that touches me withers and falls off. The shoulder mortifies. It's a very long, very slow, very entertaining form of death. So by all means, strike."

She held out her dead left hand, palm up, right in front of David, inviting him to strike.

David looked at me. I nodded. Like I was sure. Like I was doing anything more than guessing.

With a howl of pain and rage, David swung the sword high over his head and brought it down on that unflinching arm.

The blade sliced through the decayed flesh, through the bone. The hand fell to the stones.

The sword did not turn to dust.

Hel froze. We all did.

Then the hand, separated, lying there, dead bone and tattered skin, flew. Flew like a guided missile to grip David's throat.

His screams were like the sounds of a wild animal caught in a trap. Terror, unreasoning, uncontrolled, brute terror. He screamed and screamed and screamed.

Hel stood up and ripped the veil from her face. The sudden movement drew my eye. I saw her face. I bellowed in pain and fell to my knees.

"Don't look at her face!" April yelled.

"Enough of the game," Hel laughed. "Let the deeper amusements begin!"

She reached out her living hand for me. I drew back. Too slow. Unable to escape. She closed her living hand around my neck and squeezed. No breath. Blood pounding. And yet, as my brain reeled from lack of blood, as my lungs burned and heaved, I writhed in ecstasy.

Christopher broke and tried to run. Hel's tongue snapped out like a frog's, impossibly long, half living, half worm-eaten death. It wrapped like a bullwhip around Christopher's waist and drew him back.

She dropped him at her knees. He whimpered, unable to speak.

I thought of my knife, the tiny Swiss Army knife we wryly called Excalibur. The two-inch blade had been replaced with a blade of Coo-Hatch steel. Coo-Hatch steel would cut anything. So they said. It would cut Hel's arm before she could choke the life from me.

My hand found the knife in my pocket. I fumbled open the blade. All I had to do was . . . But no, how could I? I couldn't harm this precious, living flesh. This embodiment of beauty and joy and pleasure.

"Kiss me, Jalil," Hel mocked.

She drew me close, lifted me effortlessly, while at the same time allowing just a gasp of air into my lungs. Just enough to keep me conscious. Just enough so that my eyes would see her mouth, her hideous, lovely, terrifying, evil mouth. A mouth opening wide to . . .

Scream!

"Aahhhh!" Hel cried in agony.

I fell, suddenly released. Slammed hard on the stones. Leg broken? I was too confused to be sure. I rolled over and saw the sword, Galahad's sword, protruding from Hel's right thigh.

From the living, lovely flesh.

"No!" I gasped in outrage, even as my mind sought to regain balance, to break the spell, to understand.

April yanked the sword free. Red, human blood flowed from the gash in Hel's thigh.

"Can't kill what's already dead," April grated. "But you're only half dead."

She swung the big broadsword horizontally. Hel stared blankly, incapable of comprehending.

The sword passed clean through Hel's calf.

"No!" the monster screamed. She toppled over and landed so hard that chunks of decomposed flesh fell from her left shoulder, revealing stark bone in worm-filled socket.

"I am Hel! Queen of Nifleheim! Ruler of the Underworld!"

Now Hel began to fight. She was on her side, but it was the dead side uppermost. Invulnerable.

The loose dead hand had released a still-quivering David and rejoined the arm. Hel swung her dead fist at April. April swung the sword, sliced through the dead arm like chopping at a cloud. The fist stayed put and knocked April rolling across the floor.

She rolled toward the pit.

I jumped up, ran. Grabbed April's hair, the only thing I could reach, slipped, but held on.

April stopped. I fell over her, slid past, and realized that my face was now suspended over the void.

I looked down into the pit.

Horror!

It was a shaft, lit by fire. The living and the dead hung like sides of beef, disfigured, flayed, in chains, down as far as the eye could see. They were arrayed in a spiral between endless ascending coils of a snake so huge it formed a sort of walkway. The head of the snake was out of sight, far away in the darkness below. But I knew this snake. Even in Everworld there could only be one Midgard Serpent.

But above this monstrous vision hung a single person, suspended by threads so thin they might have been spiderwebs.

Senna hung helpless above Hel's own hell.

CHAPTER
XVII

I stared at her. Her eyes were glazed, unseeing, blank.

But not dead.

I yanked back. Off April. Onto my feet. Like some invisible hand was pushing me.

Hel was standing up. She rested most of her weight on the bare bone of her dead left foot. But she could not keep her balance without allowing at least some pressure on the bloody stump.

She bellowed in pain, and part of me was fiercely glad to hear it. Let the monster feel some tiny fraction of the pain she caused others.

April stared up at her, the only one of us who could meet Hel's eye. "We're walking out of here," she said. "You try and stop us, I'll slice you up like baloney."

"What sword is this?" Hel shrieked.

"It used to belong to —"

"Don't tell her," I said. "She wants to know. Don't tell her. Maybe she could counteract it or something."

April nodded. "Yeah."

"Her foot's growing back," Christopher moaned.

New bone was pushing out of the stump. New flesh was growing.

"Did you think you could kill me? I am Hel!"

"You sure are, lady," Christopher muttered.

"Stones, arise!" Hel cried. "Now comes the mercy you have all begged for. Arise, all you who died a coward's death, wash away your shame. Seize these four!"

The stones we were standing on, the wide circle of flagstones began to hinge upward, like a bunch of trapdoors.

Beneath them lay bodies, packed close together. Men, elves, dwarfs, Coo-Hatch, and other species I did not know, but mostly men. Men who had been buried alive beneath the stones, held there for who can guess how long in airless, lightless torture.

They looked more dead than alive. I saw white men whose skin was so pale it was translucent.

Black men bleached ash-gray. Years without light. Years trapped, not allowed to die.

They rose, one by one, then in greater numbers, more and more. Their hair was filthy and matted, ears and eyes blocked with dirt. Some had no eyes at all; the worms had reached them.

Up they rose, seizing this moment of hope, ready to take us or else be buried alive again.

We backed away, sliding and slipping as stones opened beneath our feet. As decayed hands reached for us. As toothless mouths croaked.

We backed up to the pit.

"David!" April threw the sword to him.

He snagged it out of the air and began hacking at the nearest of Hel's zombies. But there was no way. There were hundreds. Thousands.

"Into the pit," I yelled. "It's the only way."

"We'll die," Christopher cried.

"We'll be lucky to die," I said. "Senna's —"

"He's right," David said. "Better to die than let Hel have us."

With a last hack at a rushing man, David stepped backward into the void.

The undead men were on us in a flash. I stumbled back. Lost my balance. Fell.

Hit something. A groan. Flailed wildly, grabbed something that resisted, something strong, but no thicker than a string.

I opened my eyes. I was hanging onto the threads that held Senna.

April fell past, screaming. Christopher fell. Hit the same web of strings.

The two of us were hanging suspended above the pit, grabbing for the rough pole that held Senna immobile.

"You!" Christopher yelled.

Senna barely moved her head.

We were too close to the lip of the pit. Hands were reaching for us. Thirty, forty, fifty hands all clawed at us, strained to reach us. Hel would come. I was sure of that. She wanted us. Wanted to torture us. Wanted to bury us alive, up to our necks, or beneath the stones, or hang us from the walls of this bottomless snake pit.

Death. Death was better. Anything was better.

"Gotta drop, man," Christopher said desperately. "Gotta drop. No choice, man."

"Yeah," I agreed.

Senna whispered something.

I strained to hear over the raucous, horrible, desperate grunts and cries of the undead.

"What?"

"Kill me," Senna begged. "Don't leave me for her."

I realized I was crying, babbling incoherently, shaking. I didn't want to die. Didn't want to.

But what I'd seen. No. I couldn't let Hel take me.

I tried to yank at the knots that held Senna tight. Impossible. Nothing could break these . . .

Yes. Something could. I hung precariously, reached my free hand into my pocket, drew out the Coo-Hatch Swiss Army knife. Opened the blade.

Cut the strings holding Senna's left arm. I slipped down and found myself holding her around the neck, strangling her.

I struggled to reach the remaining strings. Couldn't even see them. Suddenly, Hel's hideous face, her half-dead, half-living, horrible, beautiful face loomed above me.

With a last lunge I sliced the strings.

Falling!

Both of us, me, Senna, spinning slowly around, falling feet down, falling past row after row of men who'd been nailed to the walls of this vast well. Nailed through hands and feet and whatever other parts amused Hel.

Some lived. Some were dead. Most seemed to be trapped forever in an inescapable suffering.

Some were bones and nothing more. A hand here, still nailed in place, a leg, a torso.

Falling! Faster, we'd fall faster, too fast soon to

see the poor, pitiful creatures. But no. We weren't falling faster. Falling, yes, but not accelerating. Not fast enough to avoid seeing those pain-wracked, despairing eyes.

The Midgard Serpent's coils wrapped down and down. They might have been glued in place. Cobwebs attached to the snake's scales. Fallen bones rested temporarily on the curved upper surface before eventually falling.

I had the horrible realization that yes, this was the same snake whose head we had seen in Loki's dungeon. How many miles away? How many miles long was this monster?

And now, if anything, we were falling more slowly. Impossible, of course. Anywhere but Everworld.

But definitely slower. Senna's blonde hair, which had been streaming straight upward, was now floating, as if blown by no more than a stiff breeze. The log she'd been strapped to spun away beneath us.

Suddenly, the rows of bodies were gone. The spiral straightened and ran more or less directly down the shaft. And still we fell.

Only now, the last of the light had faded. We were falling through absolute blackness.

I reached for Senna. Found her. Drew her close.

I needed someone to hold on to, even if it was her. Needed some small comfort in this hopeless place.

"Can you hear me?" I asked.

It took her a while to answer. Then, "Yes, I hear you, Jalil."

And then, we landed.

I was on a ladder.

Against the side of my house.

My dad was on a second ladder, just beside mine. I was holding a storm window. Handing it to him.

"Ah-ah!" I cried.

"Hey, hey, careful with that, don't scratch the paint," my dad said.

I tightened my grip on the storm window. It was big. Arched at the top. We have an old Victorian house and my dad's curse in life is his quixotic desire to keep it looking as new as it must have looked in 1893 when it was built.

He took the storm window from me and fitted it into place. My little sister Kira snapped the clips into place and made a face at me through the glass.

Was I dead? I was falling, falling forever, then nothing.

Had I hit, had I died, was I free now, was I here, back in the real world for a moment only or forever? I could barely keep my grip on the ladder. Relief washed over and through me. Relief like a cool pond to a man crawling through the desert.

What had happened? Did Hel have me? Was my unconscious body being carried to her? Was I being bound tightly, ready for the vertical burial in the road of skulls?

"Jalil, are you paying attention?"

"Yeah. Yeah, Dad. Just, um, nothing. I'm okay."

He sighed in a disapproving way. Letting me know that when it came to preserving the perfection of our house, our home, our statement to the world, and more particularly our statement to the Winfields across the street, I was a big disappointment.

"Okay. We'll finish tomorrow. People want to think we're the kind of people who only put up half their storm windows and let the whole place look shabby, well, that's just what they'll have to think." He turned sideways on the ladder to look around. "Good lord, look at that flagstone. I swear it's off by a good two inches. You can see it from up here. It looks terrible."

"Dad, the neighbors don't climb up ladders to look at our sidewalk."

"That's not the point," he said and began to climb down. "We know it's off. What the neighbors think is not the point."

"Uh-huh."

I put the ladders away in the garage. Leaned against the exposed studs and took a few deep breaths.

I was back. Home. Alive, clearly alive. That was all I knew. All I wanted to know.

I would have given anything to erase from my mind the things I had just witnessed. Those men. The pain. The face of Hel.

"Hey, hey, hang on," my dad cried. He grabbed me by the shoulders just before I collapsed. He lowered me down to the grass. I looked up at him, dazed.

"Stay right there, I'll call 911."

"No, no, Dad, no, it's nothing." I got to my feet as quickly as I could. "I was just dizzy for a second. Maybe I forgot to breathe or something."

"What do you mean, dizzy? You're going to see Doctor what's-his-name. Come on."

I started to cry. Couldn't help myself. He was so concerned. He cared about me. Loved me.

"Now what is it?" he demanded, exasperated.

"Nothing, Dad. I don't know. Maybe I need to eat or something."

He looked relieved. My father's not good with emotional outbursts. "Food. That's it. How many times I have to tell you, you're skinny, Jalil, you don't eat enough, boy. Nothing wrong with food. You come inside now."

He insisted on holding on to me, like I might fall over. And maybe I would. My mind held too much misery. I'd seen too much. How would I ever clear out my brain? How would I ever think clearly again?

My mom fed me leftover lemon-glazed chicken, green beans, and a microwaved potato. I ate and tried to forget cries of pain. Tried to forget the diametrical passions, the lust and terror that overwhelmed me each time I saw the face of Hel.

Food helped. Not enough. But I was here, with my mom, with my dad, with my little sisters, in my home. This was normal. This was real.

I slipped away and washed my hands. Seven times. Not even bothering to fight the compulsion. Then I checked the stove knobs by twisting each one to make sure it was really, truly turned off.

I found my car, parked around the corner because my folks take both spaces in the garage. Winced at the ticket on the windshield. Then drove to Barnes and Noble and practically raced to the mythology section.

I scanned the shelves. I'd seen the book I needed on a previous visit. There it was: *Encyclopedia of Hell.*

I looked up Hel. Daughter of Loki. Sister to Fenrir and the Midgard Serpent.

"Nice family Loki's got, huh?"

It was Christopher. He met my gaze and nodded mute acknowledgment. Yes, he was "here." Yes, it had all been real. Still was real.

"Hit bottom, I guess," he said. "Lights out and suddenly I'm down at the beach making out with Tama Shakowsky. And it's getting hot, and suddenly I'm seeing . . . Her. And that's the end of me making out. Maybe forever. You looking up Hel?"

"Hel and hell both," I said. "She's the one they took the word from. Hel came first. Later the Christians adopted the word. Extra 'L.'"

"It's funny, because as bad as Loki is, man, his kids are worse. How exactly are you this Calvin-Klein-underwear-model-looking god and your kids are a snake, a wolf, and a half-dead monster woman?"

"W.T.E.," I said.

"Got that right."

"There's more. If we wake up over there, I mean."

"More? More besides Hel and a bunch of zombies and a snake so big he could have three different zip codes? What else man? What else?"

"Maybe a dragon. Nidhoggr. That's his name. He lives in the lowest levels of Nifleheim. Rips apart the bodies and souls of the dead."

"Let me guess: Loki's other kid?"

"I don't think so. I think that's it for Loki. Fenrir, the big snake, and Hel."

"And I thought my family was messed up. This is like eight bus stops past bizarre, man. I mean, these are books, in a freaking Barnes and freaking Noble, and they're in a section called 'mythology,' right? As in, not real, myth. And we're reading them like they're the encyclopedia."

I looked up from the book. "You okay?"

"Me? Sure I'm okay. Why not? Part of me is going to suddenly wake up over there and realize I can't see, can't even open my eyes because I'm squashed flat under some big rock and maybe I'll stay there for years, not dead or alive, just trapped there and screaming, only no one will hear. Begging for mercy from that —"

"All right, all right. Stop," I begged. My hands had started shaking. I was crimping the pages, tearing the edges. I shut the book and shoved it back on the shelf.

"April was cool, though, huh?" Christopher said. "Unloaded on the big bitch."

"Just shut up!" I snapped.

"Gotta talk about it. I can't have that stuff in my head and just act like it's not there. I have to get hold of it."

I stood up. "And what? Make sense out of it? She's insane. Pure, distilled, hundred-proof madness. Make sense out of that. She's crazy."

Christopher laughed. "Crazy? What do you figure, Jalil, she needs some therapy? Maybe sit down for a few sessions with some kind of shrink? Or else get on the medication? Here you go, Hel, pop a few Prozac? Make sure and chew with the teeth that aren't all rotted out and filled with maggots?"

"She's the textbook definition of a psychotic, a paranoid schizophrenic," I said. "It's in her brain itself. I mean, look at her: Half her brain is probably dead. Active at some level, yes, but vastly different from the other side."

A clerk lingered at the end of the row, obviously eavesdropping.

"Let's get out of here," I said. "I don't want to advertise the fact that I'm a wacko."

We headed downstairs, past the magazine rack and outside into chill, fall air. The corner was busy, lots of cars backed up, some honking.

"Let's hit Mickey," Christopher said. "I need a burger."

"I'm not spending the day with you, Christopher. I see enough of you over there."

Christopher pointed at one of the regular street people, a very large man who alternated between angry babbling about CIA conspiracies and sweet-voiced pleas for money. "See, that's crazy. That's a messed-up mind. Guy's fried. But Hel? Uh-uh. That's not mental, that's not brain chemistry, she's just evil."

Christopher headed for McDonald's. I headed toward the Borders store nearby. Bookstores were safe. Bookstores were about reason and thought and cool, clean words on crisp white paper. Bookstores were temples to everything Everworld was not.

I spent an hour at Borders. Then caught a bagel at Einstein's. I didn't want to go home. At home the OCD grew stronger. Home was the center of all my obsessive rituals.

I wanted to be far from insanity. Hel's or mine.

The hours wore on. Each hour bringing closer the moment when part of me, a me, one of me, would awaken in a place that could not possibly exist.

I would stay here. This me. A me. One of me would stay here, unaffected. At least directly. But my mind was permanently poisoned.

"The information age," I said under my breath. "Information is power."

What a naïve little slogan. What a nice bumper sticker. You see it everywhere. But what the fools never consider is that power flows both ways. Sometimes what makes one man strong makes another weak.

Information was power. The memories, the images in my brain, the horrific, unforgettable visions, they were power all right.

Hel's.

CHAPTER XIX

Eyes open.

Absolute darkness.

I froze. No movement. *Give no sign you're awake, Jalil. Control your breathing. Listen. Listen closely.*

Did I hear anything moving? Anything breathing?

"You're very good at that."

The voice made me jump. It was so close. Familiar.

"Senna?"

"Are you hurt? I checked as best I could. I didn't feel any broken bones or anything."

I tried moving my legs. Moved my arms. Raised my head. "I'm not hurt."

"I waited for you to wake up. I could have tried to revive you, but I figured you could use some time over there. Real world. That's what you call it, right?"

I sat up. "Where are we?"

"In a deep, deep hole," Senna said. "With a very big snake."

"Does it . . . is it . . ."

"The snake? His head is miles from here. Maybe he'll come, maybe he'll pop up from some other direction, or maybe he can't even get here. I don't know. I just know the tunnel is full of snake off to the right. My right."

There's supposed to be a dragon down here somewhere," I warned.

"Nidhoggr?"

"How do you know that?"

"You talked in your sleep. I don't know if he's real or not. If he is, I guess we should try and avoid him."

I looked up. What might have been a million miles away I saw a tiny circle of dim light: the opening of the pit.

Thousands, tens of thousands of men and other creatures hung in agony, waiting for a prolonged death.

"Where are the others?"

"I don't know. No other bodies down here. No one but the two of us. They may have taken off. Or been taken."

I thought about that. "Later, maybe I'll sleep. See if I can get in touch with them in the real world, get some news."

Silence. Then, "Thanks for cutting me loose."

"I'm surprised you and Hel didn't get along," I snapped.

Senna didn't rise to the bait. "Hel doesn't have a lot of friends. Even Loki is afraid of her. Down here, down in Nifleheim, she can't be touched. The regular gods have no power down here. The only ones who can mess with Hel are the other Underworld gods: Hades, Donn, Osiris, and so on. It's why she didn't give me to Loki. Hel doesn't look to the future much."

"You told her about us."

To my surprise she reached out, fumbled, found, and then took my hand. "Whatever you want to think of me, don't think I willingly helped her. Would you have been able to resist her, had she asked you a question? Any question?"

I let go of Senna's hand. "No," I admitted. "I'd have answered any question. I'd have cut my own throat if she'd told me to."

"She has great powers," Senna said.

"Yeah? Well, I'm going to figure it out. I'm going to figure it out, figure out how it works."

I sounded ridiculous. I didn't care.

"What? What are you going to figure out?"

"Magic. Everworld has held together for a long time. So, as weird as the rules may seem, there are rules. There is a system. There is software."

"You're pretty cocky for a guy sitting in the dark in the lowest circle of Hel's kingdom."

"Not about cocky," I said softly. "Humans lived for a million years thinking the sun went around the earth. Not knowing what caused diseases. Not knowing why the wind blew or the rain fell. They called it all magic. Used to be ninety-nine percent of everything was 'magic.' Now we know."

"Ah. So you'll be the first scientist in Everworld," she said, mocking me.

"You know, for like a thousand years, people, educated people, argued over whether light came from the source, or from the eye itself. They thought maybe somehow the light was projected out of the eye and lit up the world around them."

"Kind of a charming idea, isn't it?"

"So then one guy said, 'Hey, look up at the sun.' They looked up at the sun. The sun hurt their eyes. And all at once, no one doubted that light came to the eye, not from the eye. Centuries of not knowing, till one guy came up with an experiment. And then, understanding. Truth."

Senna said nothing. The silence stretched.

"Maybe we should get going," she said at last.

I was very gratified to hear annoyance in her voice.

That's right, I thought. *I will find the key to Hel, to Loki, to Merlin, and to Huitzilopoctli. And to you, Senna the Witch. I will find the key, and open the software, and I will take this universe apart and lay all its pieces out for all to see and understand.*

Cocky? Yeah, it was. False bravado, that's what it was. But I'd take any kind of courage I could get. Because as I moved I felt my hair brush against something. I reached up and touched the edge of a single scale the size of a conference table.

The Midgard Serpent did not react. My heart did.

CHAPTER
XX

We began to walk, feeling our way carefully. Six-inch steps. Hands outstretched. Blind. Hearing was everything, and there was nothing to hear but our own breathing, our own shuffling steps.

"There should have been bones." The thought had just occurred to me.

"What?"

"All those guys hanging up there, all the way down the shaft. Over time they must rot away. I saw partial bodies. Lots of them. Thousands. Bones would fall, there should have been bones piled up where we landed. It was clean."

"Whatever you say, Jalil."

"So someone cleans up down here. Someone collects the bones and whatever else Hel tosses down here."

"Not the dragon," Senna said. "Wouldn't be the dragon. They only care about gold."

"How do you know this stuff?" I demanded.

Senna laughed softly. "Same way you do, Jalil: by paying attention to what I see and hear. Do you have any kind of weapon?"

"Excalibur," I said wryly. "The little knife I used to cut you loose. How about you? You're supposed to be a witch."

"My small powers are worth nothing down here," Senna admitted.

We started moving again, if possible with even more caution. "How did you end up here?"

"Long story," Senna said.

"I don't seem to be going anywhere. Last we see you, you're with us at Galahad's castle. Then the shooting starts and you're out of there."

"I was in a no-win situation, Jalil. If Merlin had won, he would have imprisoned me forever. If Loki had won, I would have been his slave, forced to become the gateway."

"So you took off."

"I took off." She fell silent.

"You know, somehow conversations with you never go anywhere, do they? You have a nice habit of turning commas into periods."

"We should focus on the problem at hand."

Now it was my turn to fall silent. I stopped talking. Stopped breathing. Stopped moving.

"Jalil?"

No movement. No sound. Only the beating of my heart. Could she hear that?

"Jalil!" More insistent.

"Jalil! Where are you?" Now with growing fear.

"Right here, Senna."

"What the hell were you doing?!" she snapped.

"Reminding you that without me, you are completely alone. Powerless. You said it yourself, your powers don't work down here. You're just some skinny white girl on her own in a bad, bad place."

"I'm disappointed in you, Jalil. Blackmail?"

"Screw you, Senna. I want to know how you ended up down here."

We started walking again. Hands reaching into nothingness. At any moment the ground might stop at a cliff's edge and I would never know till I was falling.

Senna said, "I needed to get far away from Merlin. Far away from Loki. I headed into the forest. It was very hard at first. I found no food, only a little water. I was afraid that I would never find a place to rest and have a moment's peace."

"Uh-huh," I offered as encouragement.

"Fortunately, I encountered a small, traveling troupe of Coo-Hatch. They fed me."

"Coo-Hatch? They fed you in exchange for what?"

"In exchange for nothing, really —"

"The Coo-Hatch are businessmen," I said. "They'll trade. I don't think they'll give."

"So you've met them." Senna laughed softly, mirthlessly. "All right, they wanted information about the real world. They had some kind of book. It looked like a human book."

In the darkness she couldn't see my expression. I gave no clue that I knew precisely what book it was: the chemistry text we had traded to the Coo-Hatch.

"Really," I said. "What did they want to know?"

"It was strange, really. Even for aliens. They all huddled around me and started asking me about guns. Weapons. You know, really technical stuff, like the shape of projectiles. What the projectiles were made of. Like I would know."

I felt a sudden stab of guilt. I'd been concerned at the time about giving the Coo-Hatch the book. The Coo-Hatch make a steel unlike anything any human has ever smelted. But the course of tech-nology runs unevenly. Just because they were geniuses with metals did not mean they knew the composition of gunpowder.

"Interesting," I said. "Then what?"

"Then I left them and set out on my own again. I was hoping to make it to a new domain. Far from Loki's reach. Then I found myself cut off by a number of horsemen. I felt I would be safer as a man than as a woman. So I . . . so I gave the horsemen the impression that I was a man. A young, strong, possibly dangerous man."

"You put some kind of spell on them?"

"I gave them an impression. A female traveling alone? They would not have hesitated to attack me."

"Except this time you were wrong," I said, grinning in the dark. "Let me guess: These particular men were not interested in rape."

"No. Hel's eunuchs, out looking for strong young men for Hel's little harem. They took me, dragged me to the city. I waited, bided my time, then resumed my normal appearance. Unfortunately, someone saw me and informed the guards. I was taken to Hel."

I wondered how much of her story was true. Senna would not hesitate to lie. Something did not ring true. Some fact was nagging at the back of my mind. Something not right.

I tried to work it through but came up empty.

"Shh!"

I froze. Listened. Sounds. Definite sounds. Muffled. A soft clanking. And a gnawing, chewing sound.

"What is it?" I asked Senna.

"I don't know. Really."

"Getting closer. Louder."

Then, a scream. Muffled. Coming from within the wall itself.

April!

CHAPTER
XXI

"It's April!" I yelled. I started tearing at the side of the cave, ripping away clods of dirt and hand-sized rocks.

"You'll bring it all down on us!" Senna snapped.

"They're behind this wall," I said.

"Jalil. Stop."

Senna put her hand on my shoulder. Sought to make contact with the bare flesh of my neck. It came to me in a flash: The sword. It shouldn't have hurt Hel.

If it was true that magic was powerless within Hel's kingdom, then why had Galahad's sword frightened Hel?

Senna had lied.

And now . . . now my hands . . . filthy. The

germs crawling, invisible but there just the same. I had to wash them. Had to wash them.

No. No, no, no, I was free of all that here. That was a real-world disease.

Senna.

I slapped her hand away.

"Jalil, I'm frightened, hold me," Senna said.

I fumbled for my knife. Drew it out, backed away in the darkness, out of Senna's reach. I opened the blade.

"Coo-Hatch steel, Senna," I said. "It cuts anything. Reach for me again, I'll see if it cuts a witch."

"You damned stupid fool!" Senna hissed. "Whatever is down here is more than a match for us. If you draw them to us, we'll die."

"You had your chance, Senna. You lied. How many lies, I don't know. Maybe Hel seized you like you said, or maybe you went to her looking for something and she double-crossed you."

Senna laughed a nasty laugh. "Oh, I told most of the truth. But once I realized where I was, I knew I could use it to my advantage. Or thought I could. She's not exactly reliable, old Hel. I wanted sanctuary. Loki can't touch me in the Underworld; neither can Merlin."

"What did you offer her?"

"What a tired immortal wants most: something new. Eternal life is a real bore, Jalil. She wanted something new."

"Us?"

"Real-world men," Senna said. "Hel's had everything else. Never a man from the real world. She was excited by the prospect of finding out what would break you, what would terrify you, what would reduce you to babbling, pathetic slavery."

It took my breath away. I had nothing to say.

"Don't act so shocked, Jalil. I wasn't going to leave you with Hel. She can be destroyed, you know. Hel can be destroyed. It would have worked, maybe. I thought I could destroy her and take her kingdom, rule in her place, a benevolent regime. End the torture. Free her victims. All those poor, poor men up there, all those people in pain, I would have freed them."

"Power. That's it for you, Senna. That's the drug for you, isn't it? You want the power. You've gone crazy with it."

"Someone will win this contest, Jalil. Merlin would imprison me. Loki would use me to invade the real world. Is that what you want? My only choice is to take control myself. You must see that. It's reasonable, Jalil — that's your drug, isn't it? Reason? Everything has to be neat and orderly and make sense? Well, it makes sense, Jalil. I'm the gateway. But I don't have to be a tool. I can be a power!"

A second scream from through the wall.

"Touch me and I'll hurt you, Senna," I said. I began digging, clawing really. Couldn't absorb what she'd told me. Too much. Not now, later.

"Your hands are awfully dirty, aren't they?" Senna sneered. "You should wash them, don't you think?"

"Shut up."

"Dirt under your fingernails, and all?"

"Doesn't work, Senna," I said. "It's not quite that easy."

"Do the others know? What a great laugh they would have. Should I tell them?"

Put her on "ignore," Jalil. Just another noise. Filter it out. Get to the others, that's what counts.

The knife. Of course. I began whipping the blade around in a sort of crude oval. It sliced through dirt and rock, an inch at a time. It was slow, but faster than digging.

Suddenly, light!

The wall collapsed. Dirt fell from the hole I'd been digging, covered my shoes up to my ankles. The light was probably dim, but blinding to me.

I stood there, blinking, shaking. "I found the missing bones," I said.

Chapter

XXII

They had dug a tunnel paralleling the one we'd been in. Vastly wider. Taller. Brighter.

The Hetwan. I saw three of them spread back along the tunnel, all too visible in light the color of dried blood.

The two weirdly jointed legs that ended in pads and made a sneakers-on-tile sound; the furled wings; the oddly human mouth being fed invisible dainties by three always-moving mouth-part claws.

The three Hetwan watched over the army of diggers. Dozens of them, maybe hundreds, spread down the length of the tunnel, widening it in every dimension, digging away with the bare bones of their hands.

In fact, with nothing but bare bones.

The diggers were skeletons. Assembled out of

mismatched bits and pieces of bone. Some were almost complete, almost whole, like they were the bones of a single person. But the others, the majority, were composed of a longer shinbone and a shorter; a thicker arm and a thinner; an elf's childlike foot and a dwarf's clunkier model. Some of the skeletons bore no clear resemblance to anything human or elf or dwarf but were like failed attempts to create a new machine entirely: Extra arms protruded from breastbones; third legs were glued onto pelvises. One skeleton drew my eye to its four strong legs. A centaur.

Some of the diggers had skulls, others not. The skulls were often broken, with missing jaws or gaping holes.

It was the diggers without skulls that were somehow most terrible: legs and arms and ribs and pelvises, all working away, digging, as though they had a will, a purpose.

"Jalil!"

I heard the voice cry out, to my right. There the diggers were clustered thickly in one area.

I heard the clang of sword on bone. The cries, grunts of effort of my friends.

"I have to go help them out," I said to Senna. "You can come or not."

There was no answer. I turned to find Senna gone. In her place, a skeleton.

"You're very good at that, Senna," I said.

I reached over, grabbed her by what looked to my enchanted eyes to be bleached arm bones, and with all my strength shoved her into the mass of diggers.

"What are you doing?" she cried, her skeleton jaw opening and closing in a parody of speech.

I didn't answer. I didn't know why I'd done it. I just knew it felt right.

"There!" One of the Hetwan raised his hand and pointed at me.

The diggers suddenly noticed me. Till then they'd been oblivious. They were not alive, I knew that. Nothing but automatons serving the will of the Hetwan.

A digger reached out a dirt-caked bony claw for me.

I whipped Excalibur down and severed the arm bone neatly. No reaction from the digger. He kept clawing at me. He was digging at me, I realized. The skeletal automatons were capable of very little. Nor were they very strong.

I shoved past him, shouldering him aside. He made a sound of china plates clacking together.

I'd lost Senna in the melee. She was one skeleton among many. Pointless fighting these automatons. They would keep going forever.

"David!" I yelled.

"Jalil! We could use some help!"

"Forget the bones, man, go for the Hetwan!"

"What Hetwan?" Christopher shouted.

They hadn't seen the masters, only the slaves. I kicked a skeleton in his third arm. The bone cracked off and fell to the ground. "Three Hetwan. On past me. They're running these things."

"Form up tight, on me," David cried.

Suddenly I could see him. He was pushing his way through the flailing skeleton diggers, slashing, hacking with his big sword. Maybe David isn't a hero but there are times when he sure looks like one.

Christopher and April, all dirty, bruised, and battered, covered his flanks, pushing the skeletons away, whipping at them with bones that had become weapons.

I swallowed the fear and distaste and forged out toward them, like trying to cross the river, kicking, pushing, slashing at bone with my tiny knife.

I stumbled into Christopher. He caught me.

"Senna," I gasped. "She's here."

"Where?"

"She's one of them." I swung my arm wide, indicating the automatons.

Christopher grabbed me and held me up to

bring his mouth to my ear. "Don't tell David, man."

He released me in time to stiff-arm a digger.

Did he want to avoid distracting David? Or was he hoping David's sword would conveniently bring an end to the problem of Senna?

I didn't care. Either way, Senna could fend for herself.

Our movement as a group confused the automatons. Or the Hetwan controlling them. They came at us, but never in concert. Had the hundreds of skeletons attacked en masse they could have overwhelmed us. But they milled and wandered and then rushed but often missed. They were like school science fair robots, not quite functional, not quite ready for the store shelves.

"It's the Hetwan," David said. "Their control isn't tight enough for this."

He was right. The Hetwan had been running the skeletons as diggers: simple, repetitive work. This was different.

In seconds we would reach the aliens. They must be able to see that. But they did not move. Did not try to escape.

David lunged suddenly and came up to the closest of the Hetwan. He shoved the point of his sword under the creature's chin.

"Back off and let these things go or I'll kill you, Hetwan," David yelled.

"My death does not matter," the Hetwan said in a whispery, flutey voice. "I serve Ka Anor."

April shoved in beside David and grabbed his arm. "What do you mean, you serve Ka Anor? What are you doing here?"

The Hetwan said nothing. His three grasping claws kept trying to snatch food out of the air.

David pulled the sword's point away and slammed the Hetwan with the handle butt. The Hetwan fell straight back, landing stiff as a board.

A portion of the diggers seemed to stall out. Slowly, they crumpled into heaps of bare bones.

"Two more to go," I said.

We forged ahead, aiming for the two remaining Hetwan. All we had to do was dispatch the two of them, which would terminate the remainder of the animated bones. Then . . . well, we'd figure out what to do then.

But we never got the chance to nail the Hetwan. Because at that moment I felt a wave of air pressure. Like being on an underground subway platform and feeling the rush of an approaching train.

The Hetwan were standing thirty yards away from us, surrounded by diggers.

Something big, something dark, something

that filled the entire tunnel came rushing up
from behind the aliens. It flattened the two Hetwan, crumpled them like they were paper bags.

It crushed rows of diggers, blasted toward us,
unstoppable.

"Down!" David yelled.

I dove, hit the dirt, stabbed myself in the thigh
on a sharp, upthrust bone, and wormed lower,
digging into human skeletons.

It swept above me, brushed my back. I was on
the train tracks as a five-car train went barreling
by overhead. That's how it felt.

Then it was past.

"What was that?" Christopher yelled.

"Who cares? Run!"

CHAPTER
XXIII

I jumped up, spun, staggered, tried to see what had almost run us down.

It wasn't a rat. I was sure of that. But rat was the first thing that popped into my head. One big rat.

It was larger than an elephant and it was turning around. The fur was spiked, like a porcupine, needles swept back away from the head. The head was two Hetwan-style eyes mounted above a mouth too full, way too full of needle-sharp teeth.

"It's Rat Fink! I swear to God, it's freaking Rat freaking Fink!" Christopher yelled.

It wasn't. But the mouth was.

"What's next? Big murdering Beanie Babies?"

"Ka Anor?" April whispered.

"Ka Anor is my master," the beast said in a

voice like wet gravel. "Great Ka Anor does not trouble himself with mortals."

"It talks?" Christopher shrilled. "It talks?!"

The shark's grin widened. "It eats, mortal. It eats."

"Here it comes!"

Ka Anor's Rat Fink rushed straight toward us. No chance to outrun it. No chance at all.

David stood firm, sword held high, pointed at the monster's face. The beast never hesitated.

The sword hit the creature between its insect eyes. Penetrated. Pale blue blood sprayed. The sword was buried, nearly up to the hilt, ripped from David's grasp.

David was down. The animal ran over him, hit Christopher, trampled him. I snatched up a thighbone, swung it futilely at the face, the gnashing mouth. Knocked down, air exploded from my lungs, what? What was. . . . Scooped up.

Teeth everywhere. All around me, above, below, a ring of teeth, sharp as daggers, ten inches long, I was going to die, to die right here, now, in the monster's mouth.

The jaw closed.

Stopped.

My trembling hand still held the thighbone. The bone jammed jaw and roof of mouth apart. The teeth stopped, inches from me. My shoulders rested back against a row of them. I felt them penetrate my clothing, my skin, knew my own blood was flowing.

Something grabbed me. Wrapped itself around me, a snake, a tongue. It pulled me down. Struggle, fight but too weak.

Down, no, no, no!

Stop, let me go, I can't die, I can't die.

Wet flesh closed around me, smothered me as I gasped and choked and screamed in silence. Smothered. Couldn't move. Only twist as the throat turned me, rotated me down toward oblivion.

My mouth was filled with the flesh of the creature. My hands glued to my sides. Muscles began to pummel me, beat me, break me up by shattering my bones, ripping cartilage from bone and flesh from cartilage.

It was beginning to digest me.

Then, something hard against my head. Hard and round. A head! Someone else had been swallowed with me.

Dead in seconds. No air. Eyes blinded, no light. Maybe I was already dead.

Maybe I . . .

My fingers felt a hard knot in my pocket. The knife! The knife, not enough time, impossible, no air, please, please let me live, the knife, open with one hand, blade out, slashing in tiny cramped motions, blackness all around me, like a vast open pit of blackness. I was falling into blackness.

Air!

Air! Impossible. A hallucination. A dying brain giving me one last, sweet illusion.

No, it was real. Air! Suck it in, breathe. I slashed the knife upward. My arm was free. My lungs were full. I fell. Light, very dim, almost nothing, just a suggestion of light, but it was enough.

I was still inside the beast. Still inside. But outside of a mass of twisted pale-blue blood vessels the size of power lines and a throbbing, pulsating mass of organs, like looking inside a human body with all the skin and bones and muscle removed, just a mass of variously shaped things that might have been hellishly large servings of raw liver.

I was inside an air bag. The outer skin of the creature was inflated around a core of organs. It was like standing inside a blimp.

I saw the blade of David's sword. It stuck through, just inches above what might have been the creature's brain. David had missed, but not by much. The wound was fast being sealed by a sticky ooze that coated the inside of the airbag.

Within the intestine I saw a vague outline. Human.

I staggered back and sliced the organ open. Like slicing the skin of a sausage. The intestine split, a burst plastic bag of rotting garbage.

April rolled out. She was covered with goo, much as I was, I now noticed.

"Come on," I said. I grabbed her hand and pulled her up. We both staggered as the animal moved, bounced into the inflated outer skin.

I sliced down.

There was a rush of wind, and suddenly we were inside a collapsing tent. I held the folds of the cut open and we stumbled and tripped back out into the tunnel.

David and Christopher were pinned beneath the evidently dead monster.

Cutting them free was dirty and difficult work. But at last we all sat together, surrounded by a landscape filled with now-inanimate bones, three unconscious Hetwan, and the collapsed remains of the monster we would forever after call Rat Fink.

We were a mess. I had five shallow puncture wounds across the back of my shoulders. David's wrist was sprained and swelling. There was blood seeping into the white of Christopher's left eye, and his back had been sandpapered. April's nose was bleeding.

We were a sorry-looking bunch. We did what we could to bind one another's wounds, but the effort ended as we simply collapsed, exhausted.

"Well," Christopher said, "this has not been our best day ever."

CHAPTER
XXIV

I realized after a while that Christopher was sending me a "significant" stare.

Only then did I remember.

"Senna was with me," I said.

"What do you mean?" David asked.

"I mean, I cut her loose from the top of the pit. She fell with me."

David jumped up. "Where is she?"

I shrugged. "I don't know. When we broke through into this tunnel she . . . I don't exactly know the word for it . . . she changed the way she looks."

"She had a makeover?" Christopher said.

Tired as we were, we laughed anyway. I said, "She can change the way she appears, I guess. She changed into one of those skeletons."

"Did she get away?" David asked anxiously.

"Don't know, man. And I don't care," I added defiantly. "Senna's a sick piece of work."

"You get an 'amen' off that, man," Christopher said.

"She sold us out to Hel."

"I don't guess Hel left her much choice," David snapped. "You saw how it was. You think Senna was Hel's best friend?"

I shook my head. "No. But Senna made a deal with Hel. Sold us out. She wanted a safe place to hide."

David scoffed. "A safe place? With Hel? You think Senna's that stupid?"

"Senna wants power," I said flatly.

"Who doesn't? Everyone in Everworld wants power. I want power. You want power. So what?"

"She set us up, you moron!" I yelled. "She sold us out because Hel is bored and on the make for new toys. Senna gave us to the evil bitch up there because she thought Hel would hide her."

April said, "Senna just walked up to Hel with that idea?"

"No," I admitted. "Hel already had her. The eunuchs grabbed her and gave her to Hel."

"Well, that's a little different, don't you think?" David said sarcastically. "When I first saw Hel I'd have made the same offer. So would you. So would any of us."

"That's not how she put it," I insisted. But I was feeling my position weaken.

"Senna would never admit she was just scared to death," April said. "She'd rather have you think she was evil than weak."

"Hey, I believe you, man," Christopher said to me.

We fell silent after that. I looked around and asked myself where the light came from in the cave, how it was that the monster we'd killed could speak, how it was that everyone in Everworld, down to the pigs in the forest, spoke English. Or maybe the question was why we could understand everyone no matter what they said, who knows?

Did light come from the sun, or does it shine out of the eye? Did everything in this lunatic asylum speak English or did I simply understand everything as being English?

One thing was fairly clear: "Ka Anor is coming after Hel."

David nodded, glad to have something on which to agree with me. "Yeah. That's what this is about down here. Ka Anor ordered this tunnel built. Gonna come up from below, up from the pit, the one direction Hel will never expect. The diggers surprised us in the dark tunnel. On us in a flash, collecting new bones, then back over here and sealed the breach behind them."

"Why would Ka Anor go to all this trouble?" April wondered. "He must have limits on what he can do. You don't go to all the trouble of digging this huge, long tunnel miles deep to sneak up on someone unless you're a little worried."

"So, maybe Merlin is right," Christopher said. "If all these gods got their stuff together, united, they might be able to take Ka Anor down."

"Ka Anor isn't all-powerful," I agreed. "He was making deals with Loki. Loki promised to give him Senna. Of course, Loki intended to double-cross Ka Anor all along."

"What makes you say that?" David asked.

I shrugged. "Loki sends the Vikings to take out Huitzilopoctli. Why? Because Big H's Aztecs must be working for Ka Anor. Loki figures if he double-crosses Ka Anor and keeps Senna for himself, then Special K is going to send the Aztecs to get Senna back. If Loki can wipe out the Aztecs, maybe even Huitzilopoctli himself, he's safer from Ka Anor; he buys himself time to figure out how to use Senna."

"Very good, Jalil." It was one of the skulls, lying in a heap of bones.

Christopher jumped about three feet, straight up, without ever even getting off his butt.

Senna stood slowly, a skeleton. Then became Senna again.

Once again, I wondered: Had she changed, or had her image in my mind changed? Sun or eye?

"Senna," David whispered.

She touched him absently, hand on his shoulder, sliding up to make casual contact with the bare skin of his neck.

"That was very clever, Jalil," Senna said calmly, as if she'd been sitting chatting with us all along. "I couldn't figure that out. Could not figure out why Loki would court trouble with Huitzilo-poctli."

"You know what I can't figure out?" April said. "How did you end up with Huitzilopoctli? I mean, we went by ship, and suddenly there you are, too."

Senna smiled at me. "Jalil knows."

"She came the same way we did," I said. "She was on one of the boats. Just didn't look like herself, that's all."

"Another makeover," Christopher grumbled.

Senna looked pityingly at him. "That was barely funny the first time."

"Now what?" April demanded harshly, pointedly looking at David.

David shook himself, like a man trying to wake up after a nap and not quite succeeding. "We . . . we get out of here. That's what."

"Not with her," April said, pointing at her half sister.

David's eyes cleared. He moved away from Senna. "April, I know how you feel, but we're basically in hell here, literally, and it may be a long time before we find a way out. We have one sword and a Swiss Army knife. Like her or don't, Senna has some powers."

It was a good argument. Even April nodded in agreement. Then she smiled.

"Give me the sword," she said.

"What?"

"Hel's whammy didn't work on me; neither will Senna's. I'm sorry, but I don't trust you boys around witches or goddesses."

To my amazement, Senna burst out laughing. "My half sister means to hack me up if I get out of line."

"I think I should hang onto the sword," David said tersely.

"I'm with April," Christopher said. "She carries the sword."

David looked at me. I nodded my own vote. Then, just so there would be no doubt, I said, "As long as Senna is with us, April's the boss."

Senna was done laughing. Her gray eyes were polar.

I smiled at her. *No, Senna, you don't scare me, not half as much as you think.*

CHAPTER
XXV

April buckled Galahad's sword around her waist.

"It works on you, April," Christopher said. "Brings out the curve of your butt."

April sighed. Looked at me, rolled her eyes a little, as if to say, *What am I doing?*

"You're the only one Senna can't convince to fall in love," I said. "It has to be you."

"Which way?" David asked, barely restraining his anger at being superseded. "The tunnel ends up that direction. That leaves going back along this Hetwan tunnel the way the Rat Fink came, or climbing the pit back up to Hel and the Midgard Serpent."

"I'll take Hetwan over Hel," Christopher said. "Then again, I'll take root canal with a Black and Decker over Hel."

"I'm with that," I agreed.

"Then lead on, April," David said sarcastically. He made a low bow, sweeping his hand toward our chosen path.

April shook her head. "I wasn't raised on war movies," she said. "I don't have the hero myth stamped on my brain, so you know what? I think I'll do what makes sense instead. Senna? Sister? You take the lead. Then me, then David, Christopher, and Jalil."

"Lock and load, Ripley," Christopher said.

We set out, Senna walking in front where four sets of eyes could watch her.

After a while we got past crunching over bones and reached relatively normal dirt and rock. And after a while the tunnel started heading upward. It made walking harder. But we wanted to go upward. Wanted it very badly.

"That guy, the guy back in the town at dinner, he said maybe you could cross to the real world from here," April said tentatively.

"He also said, 'If you live,'" I pointed out.

"I'm thinking let's not go exploring down here," Christopher said. "I'm thinking first we get the hell away from Hel."

April didn't argue. "Those poor men. Those poor, poor men back there."

"Now we know why the Vikings like a battle," I said.

"What do you mean?" David asked.

"Back in the real world I read about Hel. About Nifleheim. Know how you end up there? Die in your bed of natural causes. That's the big crime for the Vikings, man. Die in battle, you go to Valhalla: Viking heaven."

"Valhalla. Let's go there next," Christopher said brightly. "I don't know what Viking heaven would be like, but I guarantee you one thing: They'll have beer."

Hunger and thirst made themselves felt with increasing urgency as Christopher went on theorizing about the precise menu and beverage list in Valhalla.

I hadn't had a drink or eaten a bite since the inn back in Hel's harem city. And there had been a lot of adrenaline burned since then.

"Hey, Senna," Christopher yelled. "I don't suppose you can use your whim-whammies to conjure up a cold six-pack, can you?"

Senna ignored him.

"I mean, look, if you can, let's bail, head home and go into business. Start a place, call it . . . Magic Brew. I like that. We do a little advertising. Magic Brew, the witch's brew! Colder than a witch's . . . heart. How's that sound, Senna?"

No answer.

It was a tense little group. I found I was grateful to Christopher, though. He was managing to make clear our dislike for Senna while nevertheless treating her as part of our group. Acknowledging the schism, and at the same time papering it over.

Senna could have made it easier by responding. Even if she'd slammed Christopher. But Senna understood the real-world magic of humor. She knew that Christopher was attempting to redefine her. She wasn't having it.

Senna would define Senna. She always had.

Remember that, Jalil, I told myself. *It's the key to Senna. She wants control. She won't surrender control, not even for a second, not ever.*

Why? That was the question. If I ever knew that answer I might have the same power over her that she had over me.

"Shhhh," April said.

"What?"

"Listen. Water."

She was right. Almost invisible, a tiny rivulet of water poured from the rock wall to our right.

"She drinks first," April said, indicating her half sister.

Senna smirked. She cupped her hand, waited for it to fill with water, and drank deeply.

Christopher pushed in next. His hand filled with water. His mouth —

Senna said, "Persephone."

I grabbed Christopher's hand.

"What, man?" he demanded.

"Persephone," I said, meeting Senna's amused, malignant gaze. "She traveled to Hades, the Underworld. While there she ate some seeds."

"Pomegranate seeds," Senna supplied.

"And forever after she was condemned to spend part of each year in the Underworld."

Christopher backed away from the water. No one else drank. Only Senna. Senna's words had had their effect.

Senna would always look for control.

April looked troubled. She reached unconsciously for her sword, touched the hilt, reassuring herself.

We resumed marching. Quieter now.

Upward, always upward, but never at a steep-enough slope to imagine that we were rising very far. Along the way we passed other digging "implements" used by the Hetwan: the rotting corpses of large, molelike animals not much different from Rat Fink. Hetwan creatures, without a doubt. Certainly nothing from human imagination.

Why had the Hetwan switched to the barely functional, cobbled-together skeletons? Had they run out of the big moles? Was Ka Anor over-extended?

Something to consider. So much to consider. So much to understand. If I survived.

We had no way of knowing if it was night or day. No way of knowing when, if ever, we would emerge from the Underworld. No way of knowing where we were heading, except that we seemed to be heading upward.

Tortured by thirst and hunger, we trudged, ever more exhausted.

Only Senna never seemed to tire. But then she, at least, had filled her belly with water.

"The path splits up ahead here," Senna announced. "Which way should I go?"

She stopped, waited, hands ostentatiously at her sides, looking as harmless as any shark.

The tunnel split into three. The main shaft, the one we were on, went straight ahead. It had obviously bisected an existing tunnel of some sort.

We reacted to this by flopping down on whatever convenient rock or outcropping came to hand.

"Anyone have any bright ideas?" April asked wearily.

"We have no idea what's to the left or the right," I said. "It is very likely, however, that if we continue straight on we may run into more Hetwan. Maybe more Rat Finks, and maybe Ka Anor himself. This was being prepared as an invasion route."

"I heard you can drink your own pee," Christopher said. "I mean, it doesn't kill you or anything."

"That's very helpful, Christopher," David said. He got up, walked past Senna, carefully ignoring her, and walked a few feet up the right tunnel. Then came back and went up the left tunnel.

"They're both pretty dank," he reported. "But I have the vague feeling there might be fresh air coming from the right tunnel. Unfortunately, it's kind of narrow and has a low ceiling."

"How low?" Christopher asked nervously.

"I'll be able to walk upright. You'll have to stoop."

"Screw that, man," Christopher whispered.

April used the sword to wedge herself up. She checked each tunnel. "David's right. And Jalil's right: Go forward and maybe we run into Ka Anor. Which we may want to do someday, but not without food or water, sleep, more than one sword, and a shower. Not necessarily in that order. You know, personally, I'm about sick of gods."

"I knew you'd come around sooner or later, April," I teased halfheartedly.

"'Gods' plural," she corrected. "The one is enough for me."

"Personally, I'll pray to any god that serves me up a bacon double cheeseburger and a cold frosty one," Christopher said. "They throw in a hot shower and fresh clothes, I'll become a freaking priest."

"What do you say?" David asked Senna. "About which way to go."

She shook her head. "I can't tell the future. All paths lead to opportunity. And to danger."

"Well, at least we have a fortune cookie," Christopher said dryly.

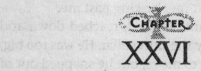

Chapter

XXVI

We stood up and walked along the right-hand path.

Then we heard it.

A rush of wind, a noise like a thousand bricks sliding down a hill, and a screaming, hissing, unnatural voice that shrieked like a tornado warning.

I was running before I knew why. Running on instinct, running on adrenaline, running from too much fear.

We all ran. No one waited to see what it was. Just ran.

But David was right, the tunnel was narrowing. I hit my head on a rock sticking down from the tunnel roof. Staggered. Legs all jelly.

I fell to my knees. Head spinning. Christopher

slammed into me, went flying, landed several feet away on his belly.

Got up, reached for support, found nothing. *Come on Jalil, move!* Staggered one step, two. Christopher wasn't moving. He was looking at me, mouth open in a silent scream, eyes bulging. No, not looking at me, looking past me.

"Come on, man!" I yelled, reached down and yanked him up by the shirt collar. He was too big, too heavy for me to move, but he snapped out of his paralysis, grabbed my arm and hauled himself up and we were running, running with that freight train shriek bearing down on us.

Only then did I turn and look. Had to see, was it her? Was it Hel?

One vast mouth, opened wide. Twin fangs, curved like sabers, each longer than I was tall. Monstrous hollow-needle snake's fangs framing a mouth of puffy pink flesh.

The Midgard Serpent raced at us, so fast! Too fast. We ran but it was like being on the train tracks and the locomotive was bearing down and there was no way, no way to outrun it.

Christopher screamed something. So did I. Our voices were lost in the rush and roar of swift death.

Then, a crunching, landslide sound. Dirt clods

showered my back and head. The impact knocked me down a second time.

I sat there, unable to run anymore. Sat there on the floor of the tunnel and stared.

The snake's garage door mouth was wide open, fangs bared. But the snake was caught in the narrowing tunnel.

"Come to me!" the snake roared in fury. And the voice was so powerful, the rage so irresistible that I found myself nearly walking toward it.

Nearly.

I stopped. Breathed for the first time in several minutes. Stared in fascinated horror at the helpless snake.

"Come to me!" it bellowed.

"I'm thinking no freaking way," Christopher panted.

"How did it get its head all the way here?" I wondered.

"Jalil, do you really, really care enough to hang around and find out?"

"No, Christopher. I really don't."

We turned and walked after the others.

We found them just a few feet away. They'd been too exhausted to run any further.

"Was it the snake?" David gasped.

"Yeah."

"What happened?"

Christopher shrugged. "We kicked its ass, man."

"Jormungand will dig out the tunnel," Senna said.

"Who's Jormungand?" April asked.

"The snake. The Midgard Serpent. It is also called Jormungand," Senna said.

Christopher laughed harshly. "Well, there's a surprise: Senna on a first-name basis with Loki's legless baby boy."

"She's right. We need to keep moving." David glanced at April. "I mean, if you say so."

"Let's move," April said. She toyed with the hilt of the sword and looked troubled. She started to unbuckle it, then stopped herself and re-cinched the belt.

"I wonder what that sword could have done to Jormungand?" Senna said. "I mean, if someone had the courage to stand and use it."

April pushed ahead, saying nothing.

The tunnel continued on uphill. It too, was lit, although less in rust red and more in a softer, grayer light.

It had to come from somewhere, this light. Unless, of course, in Everworld it really was the eye that created light.

So much to try to understand. A wondrous opportunity, in a way. Hard to focus on the joy of science though, when half your mind was occupied with considering the speed at which a gigantic snake could widen a tunnel.

Up, ever upward.

Sooner or later we had to reach the sunlight. Sooner or later we'd be out of this crushing place. Sooner or . . .

"Light!" I said.

"Light? What light?" David asked.

Everyone stopped. I pointed ahead, down the tunnel. "Ahead. Look. Ignore the background glow. There's something more like real, natural light up there."

We moved again, our steps quicker, energized by hope and by the fearful expectation that hope would be annihilated.

And yet, there was light. Light of the sun, light that could only come from the sun in the sky. Brighter and brighter.

Then, all at once, the tunnel reached an end.

Senna stopped. I walked past her, into the light. The light that was sun and gold all together. The light that reflected from a mound, perhaps three stories tall, as wide as a basketball court is long.

A mountain, an impossible mountain of gold.

Chapter
XXVII

Rubies ranging in color from cranberry juice to blood cascaded down the side of the gold mountain. Uncountable numbers of them. Rubies the size of my fists, all in a sort of stop-motion waterfall of red.

Emeralds, some as bright as spring leaves, some so dark they were almost black, some as big as fingers, others as big as footballs. Thousands of them? Tens of thousands. A pile that could have buried a garage and left no visible trace.

There was an entire section of the mountain that seemed to consist of nothing but crowns. Delicate gold circles, massive gold helmets with gold wings encrusted with jewels.

There were jeweled swords and jeweled daggers and jeweled scabbards and jeweled bowls, chalices, and plates.

But overpowering all of this, so vast, so huge that it filled the mind with images of buying entire cities, entire nations, was the gold. How many tons? How many thousands of tons? How many thousands and thousands of truckloads and trainloads and shiploads of gold coins, gold bars, gold rings, gold earrings, gold plates, gold shields, gold armor? Impossible to say. Impossible to accept that this much gold existed, all in one place.

"I think we took the right tunnel," Christopher whispered. Then he laughed, a giddy, weird, wild laugh. "Man, we could hire Bill Gates to mow the lawn."

We were in a huge, deep shaft. Like being at the bottom of a volcano. Far, far overhead the sun rode in a blue sky.

Christopher started to climb, babbling as he went. "Don't want to go out with me? How about if I buy you Jaguar. No, not 'a' Jaguar, honey, I mean the company."

Then David started climbing and so did I, so did we all, our feet treading on millions, billions of dollars.

Hand over hand, skinning knees on crowns, stubbing toes on diamonds the size of grapefruits, we climbed. Impossible not to feel elated. Impossible not to think that now, at last, all our troubles would be over, all our problems solved.

I reached the top, looked over the rim, saw that the treasure mountain was even larger than I'd thought. It flattened out, forming a sort of gold and silver and jewel plateau thirty feet or so in circumference.

And on that plateau lay a head. Reptilian skin had been covered entirely in a mosaic, swirling patterns of emeralds, rubies, and diamonds.

For a frozen moment I managed to convince myself that it was dead, that it was merely some huge bejeweled sculpture.

But then the mouth breathed. The mouth sighed, a blast of scorching air like opening an oven.

A ten-gallon tear rolled from an eye as big as a backyard trampoline.

"They've stolen my treasure," the dragon moaned pitifully. The eye seemed to notice us. The slit iris tightened.

I had seen a dragon before. A dragon had killed Galahad while we watched, helpless.

That dragon was a kitten. This dragon was Godzilla.

"The witch!" the dragon said, rolling its golden eye toward Senna. "The gateway all the immortals seek. Now they will help me recover what is mine! Now every god's hand will be turned to destroy the thieves and bring me back what I have long hoarded. Now great Nidhoggr has something to trade."

"I'm liking that other tunnel!" April yelled.

We pelted and slid down the mountain. But as we did, the mountain seemed to rise up to meet us.

The dragon was buried in the treasure! His vast tail, his oak tree claws curled up and around us, showering gold and rubies down on us like rain.

I cowered as Nidhoggr raised up his huge head, fire-dribbling mouth filling the sky above us.

April handed the sword to David.

"Nidhoggr, this is Galahad's sword!" he cried. "You know what it does to dragons!"

He was threatening to use a toothpick on a whale.

Nidhoggr laughed. The laughter was so loud it bounced the coins and hurt my ears.

"Come poke me with your puny weapon, mortal. I will lie very still. Come, come, stab at me, cut my heart out with Galahad's sword."

He laughed again, even louder. I realized I was buried up to the knees in gold. In a moment the dragon would incinerate me, and I would die a very rich man.

"You. Witch," Nidhoggr said. "I am loath to do

anything that would help Loki or his foul allies, but I will have my treasure back. And for you, Loki will bargain."

"This isn't enough treasure?" Christopher yelled incredulously.

The dragon's eye flashed. "What is mine is mine!" he bellowed. "Lo these many centuries I have held my treasures close to me, and now they are gone. The Four Talismans of the Tuatha De Danann: the Stone of Fal, which cries out at the true king; the Spear of Lugh, which brings victory to all who hold it; the Sword of Nuadhu, which no man can withstand; and most precious of all, oh, how I have loved it, cherished it . . . most precious of all, the Cauldron of the Daghdha, which brings forth the food of endless youth."

That speech left us all stunned. It was insane, of course. This dragon, this brachiosaurus of a creature, was sitting in and on enough wealth to buy France. And yet, the monstrous thing was crying, weeping swimming pools of tears.

"Nidhoggr, there's a better way," David said. "You won't have to help Loki."

The vast iris widened. "Speak, mortal with Galahad's sword."

"We'll get your treasure for you. The stone, the spear, the sword, and the cauldron. Whatever that is. We will bring them to you."

"We will?" April said.

"Maybe we better find out who took them," I suggested tersely. I was not sure I wasn't ready to give up Senna to the dragon, or Loki, or whoever else would simply take her off our hands.

"Who took the Four Talismans of the Tuatha De Danann? The filthy lurachmain, of course. The lurgadhan. Who else would dare? Who would rob Nidhoggr in his own den? None but the little thieves, the grubbers after treasure, the most vile and despicable leprechauns."

One by one, slowly, we each turned to look at Christopher.

He nodded. "Saw this coming, man. Had to be. Sooner or later, there had to be leprechauns."

EVER WORLD

#V

DISCOVER THE DESTROYER

They had taken my sword from me. Galahad's sword. My sword. Mine.

Christopher and Jalil and April, they'd told me to give it up, hand it to April. Why? Because of Senna. Because they couldn't trust me, so they said, couldn't count on me as long as she was around. How many times had I come through for them, for us all? How many times had I stood out front, not alone but out on the line, out at the point where danger pressed closest?

How many times had I been ready to give my life, to do what I had to do, and this? To be casually pushed aside with a smirk and a leer.

David can't handle Senna. David wants it too bad, man. David is hers, all hers to control, Senna's boy, Senna's pawn.

Under her spell.

I was. I knew that, and knowing that, I could fight her, resist her, even when she reached for me and touched me and I felt the power that flowed from her, the power that was sometimes so cold and demanding and sometimes so warm, so right, so . . .

I resisted her. Yes, yes, she had power. Yes, she could reach me. But I was a free man, free to say yes or no, free to make the calls as I saw them.

She was beautiful, Senna was, but it was more than that. In the real world I'd have had a dozen names for it, more excuses than explanations, really. I'd have said she was seductive, that she fascinated me, that we had some certain chemistry.

But here, in this place, this universe where the rules were all different, where nothing was what it had always been and yet was so often what it should be, here I knew the name for her power.

Magic.

She had magic. Yes, Senna the witch had power, and yet I was a free man. I was still David Levin. Senna could not change that.

And now, now with death looking down at us, death so clear and unmistakable and irresistible, now my friends gave me back the sword.

I had it back. When Nidhoggr had raised his ten-times-tyrannosaurus head up from the mountain of gold, April had handed it back without a word.

I held it now. Held the hilt that would burn some men's hands, held it tight, the blade down at an angle, pointing down toward more wealth than I could imagine.

I had tried to kill a dragon once — and failed. Failed so completely that the dragon barely noticed my presence.

That dragon that I could not kill might have been Nidhoggr's puppy.

The idea of attacking this blue-whale–sized, diamond-armored monster was a sick joke. I was a mosquito and Galahad's sword was my stinger. If Nidhoggr had chosen to lie there passively, immobile, allowing me all the time I needed, I might, might, in a long day of backbreaking effort, have managed to hack my way into one of his vital organs. If Nidhoggr were in a coma, I might have managed to kill him. But alive, alert? No.

And yet, I had the sword again. And with the sword came the responsibility, the unspoken demand to "do something."

Here you go, David. We're screwed now, so be the hero again. You die first.

It made me mad. Resentful. Now, when there was not a single damned thing I or anyone else could do; now, when the sword was as much use as a salad fork; now, suddenly, it was mine again.

Do something, David. We trust you again. Here: Take the sword and go kick Godzilla's butt.

But my resentment was tempered by a couple of facts. First, the overwhelming knowledge that our lives were entirely in the claws of Nidhoggr. Second, the fact that we were standing atop a pile of treasure so vast that to count it I'd have to figure out what word came after "gazillion."

We were going to be sacrificed on an altar worth more than many major countries. And the strangeness of that coming as it did directly on the heels of our escape from the half-living, half-dead, all-dangerous Hel and her charming brother, the Midgard Serpent, took some of the steam out of my personal resentments.

And coming slowly through the fog in my brain was the realization that we were now bargaining with Nidhoggr.

Nidhoggr had been robbed. Four items had been taken from his treasure. A stone, a spear, a sword, and a cauldron were missing. They were special. Magic. And yet a part of me, some echo of my old-fashioned, ranting socialist grandfather was outraged. I mean, how much treasure does any one dragon need?

We stood there, the five of us, on a three-story, block-long mesa, a plateau of gold, diamonds, emeralds, rubies, crowns, scepters, armor, swords, and assorted fantastic bric-a-brac. We stood there — five dumb kids from north of Chicago — and stared up at a dragon so big he could have eaten Wrigley Field in about as many bites as it'd take me to eat a hot dog, and actually heard him cry in rage as he denounced the leprechauns.

Leprechauns had stolen his stuff.

And that's when I volunteered to get his stuff back for him. The alternatives weren't good: Nidhoggr could eat us, or Nidhoggr could incinerate us. Or we could make a deal.

"What the hell are you talking about?" Christopher demanded. "Leprechauns? We're going to go get this guy's magic soup bowl back from the leprechauns? What are you, nuts? Can't we just take a rest somewhere?"

I looked at Christopher. Waited till he returned my stare. "Christopher, leprechauns are very little. This dragon is very big."

Christopher blinked. "You make a good point," he said.

"I . . . I thought leprechauns made shoes," April said.

"Old World nonsense," Nidhoggr rumbled in a low mutter that nearly made my ears bleed. "In the old times all the fairies were under control. The druids checked them. The Fianna limited their power. And of course the great gods themselves held their mischief in check. Oh, in the old times none of the fairy folk would have dared to steal from Nidhoggr! The Daghdha would not have allowed it!"

"The Daghdha?" April repeated and looked at Jalil, who shrugged. "Who is the Daghdha?"

"The great father god of the Celts, ignorant blasphemers!"

"So where is he? Maybe he could get your treasure back."

Nidhoggr seemed just the slightest bit embarrassed by the question. The man-high iris of his nearest eye narrowed a few degrees. "The stolen goods belonged to the Daghdha. They . . . came to me, after the Daghdha was eaten by Ka Anor."

"Uh-huh," Christopher said. "That clears it all up for me. Let's get going, hi-ho, hi-ho, it's off to fairy land we go. No problem. We'll get your stuff."

"Nidhoggr is not a fool," the dragon said. "You say you will bring me back what is rightfully mine. But I require something more binding than your word alone."

"I could leave you my backpack," April suggested.

Nidhoggr smiled and showed teeth silhouetted by the red magma, the burning napalm inside his throat. "I have a better idea."

Suddenly, from the ground before us, up from the mass of gold rose four figures. Like trolls, thick-limbed, thick-armed, but smaller. Or did they just look smaller with Nidhoggr as a backdrop?

Each held in his rough paws a ruby, glittering, bloodred. Each was the size of a fist. Larger. The size of a human heart.

The trolls held them out so that the rubies lay in their palms, like offerings.

"You're going to pay us?" Jalil wondered.

Nidhoggr laughed. The noise of his laughter became a physical force that sucked the air out of my lungs.

And then, as we watched with horrified fascination, the four rubies began to beat. Beat. Beat.

And inside my chest I felt a sudden stillness. A quiet, an absence no man has ever felt and lived to tell of.

My heart, my living, beating heart was in the hands of Nidhoggr's troll.

"The stones will give you life for six days," Nidhoggr said. "Return in six days with my treasure, and you may take your hearts again."

"Six days, we don't have any way, I mean, what, what if it takes longer than that?" April demanded.

"In six days the ruby in your chests will burn with Nidhoggr's own fire. Serve me well, and live. Fail me, and die."

Four rubies exchanged for four hearts. Only Senna stood unchanged. I wondered why. I knew the answer would terrify me.

"Go. Bring what is mine."